Sliding into Home

Sliding into Home

dori
hillestad
butler

Ω
PEACHTREE
ATLANTA

₽
JR
A Peachtree Junior Publication

Published by
PEACHTREE PUBLISHERS
1700 Chattahoochee Avenue
Atlanta, Georgia 30318-2112

www.peachtree-online.com

Text © 2003 by Dori Hillestad Butler
Jacket Illustration © 2003 by Paul Casale

First trade paperback edition published March 2005

Book and cover design by Loraine M. Joyner
Composition by Melanie McMahon Ives

Manufactured in the United States of America

10 9 8 7 6 5 4 3   (hardcover edition)
10 9 8 7 6 5 4 3   (trade paperback edition)

Library of Congress Cataloging-in-Publication Data

Butler, Dori Hillestad.
    Sliding into home / written by Dori Butler ; cover illustration by
Paul Casale -- 1st ed.
        p. cm.
    Summary: When thirteen-year-old Joelle, a star baseball player, moves to a new town where the only option for girls is softball, she starts an all-girl baseball league against the wishes of her school coaches and others in the town.

    ISBN 1-56145-222-X (hardcover)
    ISBN 1-56145-341-2 (trade paperback)
    [1. Baseball--Fiction. 2. Sex role--Fiction. 3. Schools--Fiction. 4. Moving, Household--Fiction.]   I. Casale, Paul, ill. II. Title.
    PZ7.B977423 Sl 2003
    [Fic]--dc21   2002015614

For Lisa,
because this book is a first for both of us

Special thanks to
Steve Janelle, Deb Bettencourt, Sarah Feeley,
and the Pawtucket Slaterettes Girls Baseball League

Chapter One

Y ou're up, Joelle!"

Thirteen-year-old Joelle Cunningham wiped her damp palms on her gym pants and walked over to the plate. The brisk March wind was cold. She shouldn't be sweating. But she was. Every girl in the entire gym class was staring at her. Joelle could feel their eyes boring holes into her back.

She couldn't blame them. After all, they didn't know her. They had no idea whether she'd slam the ball into left field or strike out.

She was the New Girl. Was there anything worse than changing schools in the middle of the year?

Joelle took a deep breath and picked up the aluminum bat. She tapped it against home plate a couple of times and brought it up over her shoulder. It was a bigger bat than she was used to. Heavier, too.

She carefully adjusted her grip. Then she changed her position a bit. Closer to the plate. No, a little further away.

The girl on the pitcher's mound tossed the ball from one hand to another, her wispy brown hair blowing in the breeze. "You ready?"

Joelle nodded. She bent her knees and squeezed her fingers tighter around the unfamiliar bat.

The pitcher took a step forward and released a fast pitch underhand.

It wasn't the angle Joelle was used to, but it came in at the height she liked. She pulled her bat back and swung hard.

Whack!

"Whoa," said one of the girls on the bench.

The ball sailed between first and second base and all the way to the street, where it dropped to the ground and rolled along the curb. *Not bad,* Joelle thought, as two outfielders took off after it.

Joelle dropped the bat and sprinted toward first base. She glanced over her shoulder as she rounded second and saw one of the fielders, a tall, gangly girl, bend down and scoop up the ball. *Yikes. Better get moving.*

"Come on, Kate!" the shortstop yelled. "Throw it here!" She waved her glove.

Should I stop at third or go for home? Joelle wondered. But Kate had only gotten the ball about halfway to the shortstop. The ball rolled on the ground and several girls ran toward it.

Home, Joelle decided, and poured on the steam.

"All right!" A girl with a bouncy blond ponytail cheered as Joelle crossed home plate.

"Way to go!" Another girl slapped her on the back.

"Thanks," Joelle said. She was a little out of breath, but she felt good.

The gym teacher, Ms. Fenner, tossed Joelle a towel. "That was some hit," she said.

"Thanks," Joelle said again, patting the towel against her damp forehead.

She was disappointed when the bell rang a few moments later, ending P.E. Most of the girls took off for the school building, but a few hung back to walk with Joelle.

"Hey, I knew you were good, but I didn't know you were that good!" Elizabeth Shaw said. Elizabeth lived in the house behind Joelle's. She and her dad had been out tossing a baseball around on Saturday, the day Joelle's family moved to Greendale. Joelle went over and threw a few with them until her mom made her come back and help unpack. Then this morning, Elizabeth had turned up on Joelle's doorstep to walk with her to school.

Joelle grinned. "I'm okay, I guess."

The girl with the blond ponytail wedged herself in between Joelle and Elizabeth as they headed toward the school. "You mean you always hit like that?" she asked.

Joelle hesitated. What could she say? She didn't usually play softball. But yeah, she was a decent hitter. Not a bad fielder, either. Her older brother Jason, who was now playing baseball for the University of Minnesota, had taught her everything she knew. "I do have a pretty good batting average," she admitted.

"Looks like our softball team just got lucky, then," said a girl with straight brown hair and a splash of freckles across her nose. "And hey, we're having tryouts after school today. Perfect timing, huh?"

"That's right," Ms. Fenner said, coming up behind the group. "They'll be at the same field where we just had class. Hope you can make it, Joelle."

"*Can* you?" the blond girl wanted to know.

Joelle glanced at Elizabeth. Her new friend had already tried to talk her into going out for softball. *It'll be a great way to meet people,* Elizabeth had said. Which was true. Except softball wasn't Joelle's game.

"Well…" Joelle began. She had to admit, she was kind of enjoying all this attention. But she was going to have to tell these girls the truth. "Actually, I play baseball," she said.

"Baseball?" The blond girl frowned.

"But only boys play on the Hoover baseball team," Freckle Girl put in.

"Hey, you saw Joelle hit." Elizabeth leaned forward. "She's really good. Definitely good enough to play with the guys!"

Joelle cringed. It wasn't a matter of being "good enough" to play with a bunch of guys. Baseball was just her sport.

"I played at my old school in Minneapolis," Joelle said.

"Didn't you have a softball team?" Freckle Girl asked.

Joelle nodded. "Sure. But I always played baseball."

"Unfortunately, I don't think baseball is going to be an option for you here," Ms. Fenner said quietly.

"Not an option?" Joelle repeated. "Why not?"

"Because there's a rule in this district that says schools have to offer the same number of boys' sports as they do girls' sports," Ms. Fenner explained.

What does that have to do with my playing baseball? Joelle wondered.

"Baseball," Ms. Fenner went on, "is considered a boys' sport here in Greendale and softball is considered a girls' sport."

Joelle still didn't get it. "You mean I can't play baseball because I'm a girl?" she asked.

"But Ms. Fenner, what about that girl Tracy who played on the football team a few years ago?" the blond girl asked. "Football isn't exactly a girls' sport."

"No, Brooke, not usually," Ms. Fenner agreed. "That's why Tracy was able to play on the boys' team. The district rule says that if there isn't an alternative sport available, coaches have to give girls a chance to play that sport. There is no girls' alternative to football. In the case of baseball, however..." She turned to Joelle and her voice trailed away.

Joelle stopped in her tracks. "But softball isn't the same as baseball!" she protested. "You play with a bigger ball in softball. A bigger bat, too. You have to pitch underhand. And you can't slide. At least not in slowpitch." That was the kind of softball the girls played at her old school.

Ms. Fenner touched Joelle's shoulder, urging her to keep walking. "I know what you're saying, Joelle. And for the record, I agree with you. But I've been teaching in Greendale for twenty years. I've seen a few girls like you, who wanted to play baseball instead of softball. I'm afraid none of them was even given a tryout."

Joelle couldn't believe it. "Why not?"

Ms. Fenner shrugged. "Like I said, district policy."

Well, this policy is about to be broken, Joelle told herself. *Once the Hoover baseball coach sees what I can do, he'll have to let me play.* Last year she'd batted almost .375. And Coach Perry said she was one of the best first basemen he'd ever had. She was tall and thin and she had good instincts. She was also left-handed, which meant she could catch throws that other first basemen often missed.

"Don't worry. We have a pretty good softball team," Brooke said, looking over at Freckle Girl. "Right, Amy?"

"Tons better than our baseball team," Amy snorted.

"We would've gone on to the district championship last year if it wasn't for Greendale Academy," Brooke added.

"That's a private school on the other side of town," Elizabeth whispered to Joelle.

"Pretty bad, huh? We were beaten by our own town," Amy said.

"They always beat us." Elizabeth sighed.

"Well, if Joelle plays on our team this year, we might beat them." Brooke flashed a mouthful of perfect teeth. "She'll be our secret weapon!"

Joelle shook her head. "Sorry. I really do want to play baseball."

"But you heard Ms. Fenner," Elizabeth said as she pulled open the door to the school. "They won't let you."

"Mmmm," Joelle said. "We'll see about that."

She wasn't going to let anyone talk her out of baseball.

No way.

* * *

Right after school, Elizabeth and Joelle headed out to the practice fields together. "See that guy over there with the blue cap?" Elizabeth pointed to a man with gray hair and a gut that spilled over his pants.

6

"That's the baseball coach?" Joelle asked. The man didn't look like he could run even one lap. But she could tell by the way he was yelling at the runner on first that he was clearly in charge.

"Yup. That's good ol' Coach Carlyle," Elizabeth said. "He's also the boys' gym teacher. And he's pretty tough. If any of them forget their gym shorts, he makes them do a hundred push-ups."

"Wow," Joelle said. He sounded a lot tougher than Coach Perry back in Minneapolis.

Joelle watched the boy who'd just gotten chewed out. He picked up the bat and got into position. When the ball came whizzing toward him, he swung. But the pitch was high, so he just nicked the ball. It ricocheted out of bounds.

Coach Carlyle threw up his hands in disgust. The kid tossed the bat on the ground and went to the end of the line.

"Are you sure you don't want to come with me to softball tryouts instead?" Elizabeth asked, squinting in the bright sun.

Joelle shook her head. "I don't mind a tough coach. Tough coaches make you work harder."

"Well," Elizabeth said, "good luck then."

"Good luck to you, too. See you later." Joelle took a deep breath and headed toward the baseball field.

The next batter hit a grounder straight between first and second. The shortstop reached down, but he didn't get his glove to the ground. The ball rolled right between his legs.

The first baseman looked a little better. A ball was hit in his direction, but it was high and way to the right. He managed to snag it easily while still keeping one foot on base. *That guy can stretch like a really tall rubber band,* Joelle thought. She could stretch well, too, but not like that. And he was going to be her competition for first base.

"Hey, you!" a gruff voice yelled.

Joelle jumped, a bit startled.

The coach was waving at her. "Softball tryouts are over on the other diamond," he said, pointing. Then he turned his attention back to the boys.

Joelle swallowed hard. Her heart pounded, but she continued walking toward the coach.

"I'm, uh, here to try out for baseball," she said when she reached him. She held out her hand. It shook a little. "I'm Joelle Cunningham."

The coach looked down at her hand and frowned. "This is a boys' team," he said. "You want to play, you go play softball. On the girls' field."

Some of the boys were staring at her now. One of them even snickered.

Joelle let her hand drop. "Actually, I'm a baseball player," she said. "I played first base at my old school in Minneapolis."

Coach Carlyle didn't answer. He just kept frowning.

"I'd just like a tryout," Joelle said, trying to stay cool. She couldn't wait to show this guy what she could do. The coach shook his head. "Sorry, young lady. Boys only on this team."

"But—" Joelle began.

The coach sighed. "Look, I'm sorry," he said again. "I really am. But I don't have time for this discussion. I've got a team to run. You want to play ball, you go see Ms. Fenner."

Joelle stood in shocked silence as the man strode away. *This is the twenty-first century,* she said to herself. *Girls can play whatever sport they want.*

What kind of backward place had her parents brought her to?

Chapter Two

But I still don't get it," Joelle told the principal later that afternoon. She was trying hard to stay calm as she sat in Mr. White's office and listened to him explain why she couldn't play baseball.

"As long as there is an alternative sport available, Coach Carlyle is not required to give you a tryout," Mr. White repeated.

"Softball isn't really an alternative to baseball, sir," Joelle pointed out. "They're totally different sports." Why couldn't this grouchy old principal see that?

Mr. White carefully stacked some papers on his desk. "I'm sorry, but that's simply the way it is." He didn't look a bit sorry.

"How can they do that?" Joelle muttered, slumping back in her chair and crossing her arms.

The principal's eyebrows shot up. "Excuse me?"

"I mean, not allowing girls to play ball?" Joelle said. "That's like something out of the Dark Ages."

Mr. White rubbed his bald spot. "Listen, um—what's your name again?"

"Joelle."

"Joelle," Mr. White said. "No one ever said you couldn't play ball. We have a fine softball program here at Hoover and—"

"But I don't want to play softball. I want to play *baseball!*"

"And why is that?" the principal asked.

Why? Joelle blinked. Did anybody ever ask any of the boys why *they* wanted to play baseball?

"What do you think you might get out of baseball that you wouldn't get out of softball?" Mr. White pressed.

"I-I've just always played baseball," Joelle stammered. This was nuts. She'd never had to explain herself before. "I like it better, I guess."

Mr. White leaned forward across his desk. "And what is it exactly that you like better about it? The boys?"

Joelle's jaw dropped. Did the principal think she was some stupid, boy-crazy girl?

She squeezed her hands into fists, then released them. "I'm a pretty good baseball player, Mr. White. Like I said, I played first base at my old school."

"I'm sure you did," Mr. White said, glancing at his watch. He stood up. "But we don't put the good players on the baseball team and the not-so-good players on the softball team. That's not the way it works."

Joelle leaned forward in her chair. "That's because softball and baseball are two different sports, right?" Now she was getting somewhere!

Mr. White put up his hand. "I'm sorry, Joanne—er, Joelle—but in this district boys play baseball and girls play softball. That's just the way it is."

11

"But that's not *fair!*"

"Of course it's fair!" Mr. White took his suit coat from the back of his chair. "We offer the same number of sports for girls as we do for boys. Do you know what would happen if we allowed both boys and girls to play on the baseball team?" He paused. "We'd have to cut a girls' sport."

"Why?" Joelle asked. Her head was spinning now. Nothing she had heard so far made any sense at all.

Mr. White frowned. "Look here, young lady. I don't much care for your attitude."

Joelle clamped her jaws together. She didn't much care for *his* attitude, either. But he was the principal. And she was just a student. A *new* student.

Mr. White checked his watch again. "And I don't have time to discuss this any further. I'm already late for a meeting. But if you want to play ball, go talk to Ms. Fenner. I'm sure she'd be delighted to have you on her team." He opened the door and waited for her to leave.

There was no point in trying to argue with the principal anymore, Joelle realized. She was getting absolutely nowhere.

She nodded and dragged herself out the door.

* * *

"I'm really sorry, Joelle," Elizabeth said as she and Joelle walked home together.

"Well, I guess I was warned," Joelle grumbled as she kicked a pebble in her path.

"I bet you could still join softball," Elizabeth said. "Maybe if you talked to Ms. Fenner first thing tomorrow—"

Joelle threw up her hands. "Why does everyone in this whole town keep trying to make me play softball?"

Elizabeth stopped walking. "I-I'm sorry," she said, a hurt look on her face. "I was just trying to help."

Joelle sighed. She hadn't meant to snap at her friend. "No, I'm sorry," she said quickly. "It's not your fault. I'm just…frustrated, you know?"

They started walking again. "I heard all that stuff Ms. Fenner said after P.E.," Joelle said. "I just didn't believe it. I was so sure Coach Carlyle would let me try out."

Elizabeth shook her head. "Maybe another coach, but not Carlyle. He probably wouldn't even let his own daughter play baseball."

"He has a daughter?" Joelle asked.

Elizabeth shrugged. "I don't know. He's got two sons, though. Two very *cute* sons." She grinned. "Eric's at Greendale High. And Ryan's in our class. He has social studies with you. I saw him come out behind you this morning."

"Oh," Joelle said. "Right." She could hardly remember even going to social studies, much less who was in the class. She had too many other things on her mind.

A few minutes later the girls reached Joelle's house. "Do you want to come in for a while?" Joelle asked.

Elizabeth checked her watch. "Well, I would, but my dad'll be home soon. I should probably start supper."

"You cook?" Joelle raised an eyebrow in surprise.

"Some," Elizabeth admitted. "I don't mind, though. It's just me and my dad, anyway. And I kind of like cooking."

13

Joelle knew Elizabeth didn't have any brothers or sisters. She wasn't sure what the story was with Elizabeth's mom. There clearly wasn't a mom around, but Elizabeth had never said why.

"I'll see you tomorrow." Elizabeth waved.

Joelle nodded and slid her key into the lock. She pushed open the front door and stepped inside.

This place sure didn't feel like home. It was too new. And too…white. Every single room in the whole house was white with beige carpeting. Maybe it would be better when all the boxes were gone and the pictures were up and the windows had curtains instead of disposable paper shades.

But she doubted it.

Joelle dropped her backpack in the entryway and kicked off her tennis shoes. What a day! She headed into the living room, flopped down on the couch, and put her feet up on one of the moving boxes.

"We're all going to be so happy here," Mom had said last week. "You know, Joelle, your dad and I both grew up in small towns like Greendale. Once you settle in, you'll see how nice it is to live in a place like this."

Yeah, right, Joelle said to herself. *Living in a little town like this is just what I've always dreamed of.* She thought about her friend Eric back in Minneapolis. He was probably at baseball practice right this minute. And her brother Jason. He was in college, but if they had stayed there at least they could have seen him on weekends. Now they'd be lucky to see him on holidays. But her parents didn't seem too upset about that.

"Jason's eighteen," her mom had told her. "He needs to

lead his own life now. You'll find a place for yourself here, too, Joelle. Wait and see."

Ha! Joelle thought. There was no place for her here if she couldn't play baseball.

She wandered upstairs to her room. She only had a couple of boxes left to unpack. Mostly odds and ends, things from Jason's old room that he hadn't taken with him to his off-campus apartment: old pennants, a baseball bank, the big stuffed banana he'd won at the state fair.

Joelle flopped down on her bed and picked up the baseball she always kept on her bedside table next to her clock radio. This was the home-run ball from the state tournament two years ago. The home-run ball that Jason had hit and *Joelle* had caught in the stands!

It was an amazing catch. Of course, Joelle always sat in line with the shortstop at Jason's games. She knew her brother's homers usually sailed right over the shortstop's head. But still, the odds of his hitting a homer right at Joelle during a playoff game—and her actually catching it—had to be about a zillion to one.

Joelle traced the thread of the ball with her finger. Everybody in south Minneapolis knew Jason Cunningham and his kid sister Joelle. Here, nobody had ever heard of either of them. It was a lonely feeling. Joelle would give anything to talk to her brother right now, like she used to every day.

She sat up quickly. Hey, why *couldn't* she call him? It was long distance, but her parents had promised she could talk to Jason as often as she wanted.

Joelle leaped off the bed and ran across the hall to her parents' bedroom. She dodged the moving boxes and finally located the phone on the floor.

Just punching in Jason's number made Joelle feel better. Her brother knew how she felt about playing baseball. Maybe he'd even have some ideas for how she could change that coach's mind.

But the phone rang three...four...five times, and then an answering machine clicked on. "Hey, we're either out or we're busy," a strange voice said. It definitely wasn't Jason's. "Leave a message and we'll get back to you."

Joelle's heart sank. Obviously her brother had more important things to do than talk to her. She hung up without leaving a message.

* * *

"So, how was everyone's day?" Dad said cheerfully as the three of them sat down to dinner. Steam rose from the take-out cartons in the middle of the table. Even without looking, Joelle knew it was chicken chow mein and beef with broccoli.

"Just fine," Mom replied. "I wasn't at my desk ten minutes before Noreen dropped a huge pile of briefs on my desk." Joelle's mother was a paralegal. Today had been her first day at the new law office. Joelle's dad managed a Bear Foods store. His supervisor back in Minneapolis had offered him his own store in Greendale, which was why the family had moved here.

16

"Good," Dad said, helping himself to the chow mein. "I have to say, it sure is nice being home at six o'clock."

"No more long commute," Mom said with a smile. She passed the carton of rice to Joelle. "So how about you, honey? How was your day?"

"Yeah, how does the new baseball team look?" Dad asked.

"I wouldn't know," Joelle said glumly as she dug into the rice. "The coach didn't let me hang around too long."

Dad's chopsticks stopped halfway to his mouth. "What do you mean, the coach didn't let you hang around? You made the team, didn't you?"

Joelle shook her head. "I didn't get to try out."

"What?" Dad asked.

"Why not?" Mom asked.

Joelle shrugged and dumped some beef with broccoli onto her plate. "As long as there's a softball team at Hoover, I can't play baseball." She slammed the carton down, splashing brown sauce on her wrist.

Dad pushed his glasses up on his nose. "You can't be serious."

Joelle licked the sauce off her wrist. "If I wanted to play football, they'd have to let me try out because they don't have a girls' football team. But since Hoover has a softball team, they don't have to let me try out for baseball."

"But that's ridiculous," Dad said. "Softball and baseball aren't the same sport."

"That's what I told them." Joelle repeated to her parents everything Ms. Fenner, Coach Carlyle, and Mr. White had said.

"So I don't get it," she finished. "Mr. White says if they start letting girls play baseball, then they'll have to drop a girls' sport. How is that fair?"

"Well, I don't know. I guess you'd have to bring that up with the school board or the superintendent," Dad said.

"Is that the person who makes all the school rules?" Joelle asked.

"Basically," Dad replied. "At least he enforces them."

Joelle chewed thoughtfully. "Okay. Maybe I should talk to the superintendent, then," she said. "If I could show him that softball and baseball are different, then they might let me play, right?"

"Hold on a minute, Joelle," Mom said. "I'm not sure you want to go to the superintendent."

"Why not?" Joelle asked.

"Yes, why not?" Dad echoed. He looked surprised.

"Well, we're new here," Mom said slowly. "And this is a small town. How will it look if we run down to the superintendent's office right away and start complaining?"

"It'll look like Joelle's really serious about playing baseball," Dad said. He wiped his mouth. "If there's a district policy that says girls can't play baseball, we'll never get around it at the school level. We'll have to go higher."

"I can't live in a town where they won't let me play baseball, Mom," Joelle said.

Mom sighed. "I know baseball is important to you, honey." She looked at Dad. "Maybe Joelle's right. I suppose it can't hurt to at least talk to the superintendent. I just don't want people to get the wrong impression. They don't know us and—"

"That's exactly the problem," Joelle broke in. "If they knew me—or if they knew Jason, anyway—they'd never try to stop me from playing."

"I think the school district administration building is down the street from my store. I'll see if I can make time to go over there later this week, okay, Joelle?" Dad asked.

Later this week? Baseball tryouts were already over! Joelle didn't have time to mess around. She had to get on the team *now*. "Maybe I should just go by myself," Joelle said. "Tomorrow after school."

"By yourself?" Mom nearly choked on a piece of broccoli.

"Sure," Joelle said, shrugging. "I'm not a baby or anything."

"I'm sure Joelle can handle it, Lynn," Dad said. "Greendale isn't Minneapolis. In fact, it might even be better this way. Let her plead her own case."

Mom thought for a minute. "Well, okay," she agreed finally. "I suppose another advantage to living in a small town is that Joelle can have a little more independence."

"That's right." Dad smiled and turned to Joelle. "If anyone can convince the superintendent to take another look at the rules, you can, honey."

Joelle grinned at the pride in her dad's voice. *It's true,* she thought. *I can do this.*

It wasn't like she was asking for anything unreasonable.

All she wanted was a chance to play baseball.

Chapter Three

Joelle's alarm went off at six o'clock sharp the next morning. She groaned as she rolled over. She was tempted to hit the snooze button, but then she wouldn't get her morning jog in. Even if she wasn't officially on the Hoover baseball team yet, she had to keep in shape.

She switched off her alarm, yawned, and dragged herself out of bed. Then she pulled on a pair of sweats and Jason's old Twins sweatshirt. After a quick glass of orange juice and a few stretching exercises in the front yard, she set off down Morgan Road.

Greendale didn't have much of a downtown. Not in comparison to Minneapolis, anyway. But there was a grassy area in the middle of a group of shops—the Town Square, Dad called it. That was where Joelle headed.

The sun warmed Joelle's back as she jogged through town. A heavy dew blanketed the grass and car windshields. The day smelled fresh and clean. *That's one good thing about moving to Greendale,* Joelle thought. *It's definitely warmer here than it was back home. There was still snow on the ground when we left Minneapolis.*

As Joelle neared the corner of First and Main, she passed a post office and a bakery. Her mouth watered as she breathed in the sweet aroma of fresh-baked donuts. *Later,* she told herself.

She kept an easy pace as she jogged around the Square. Her dad's store was just a block or two down Main Street. As she jogged past the entrance to a small park, the gray statue in the middle of the park caught her eye. It was a man sitting down, leaning his chin on his fist. He seemed to be thinking hard about something.

Joelle was so busy looking at the statue that she didn't notice another jogger rounding the corner in front of her.

"Hey, wake up!" the person called.

"What? Oops!" Joelle jumped aside.

The boy running toward her stumbled a little as he tried to avoid a collision. He was wearing a gray Hoover sweatsuit and he looked about Joelle's age.

"Sorry," she said as the runner regained his balance and jogged past her.

"No problem," he called over his shoulder.

Joelle wiped a few drops of sweat from her forehead and turned to look at the boy again. He seemed familiar. Tall, with blond hair that was long on top and shaved up the back. Then she remembered. The rubber-band guy from baseball tryouts yesterday. The one who played first base. *Her* position.

Joelle frowned and continued her jog. She wasn't going to think about that right now.

When she got home half an hour later, her parents were dressed for work and reading the paper at the kitchen table. The smell of freshly brewed coffee hung in the air.

"Wow, you guys never hung around like this in the morning before," Joelle commented. She grabbed the towel that was hanging from the stove handle and wiped it across her face.

"That's because we never had time before," Dad said.

"Not with a forty-five minute commute ahead of us," Mom added. She shook her head. "Joelle, please don't use the dish towel as a sweat towel."

"I'll put it in the hamper," Joelle said. She went upstairs to shower and dress.

When she returned to the kitchen, her parents were getting ready to leave.

"Joelle, I checked my schedule for today," Dad said. "I could probably get away for an hour or so after school if you want me to go with you to the superintendent's office."

"You don't have to," Joelle said as she poured herself a bowl of cereal. "I can handle it by myself."

"Are you sure?" Mom asked, sounding a little doubtful.

"I'm sure," Joelle said.

"Well, I looked up the address for you." Dad slid a scrap of paper across the table to Joelle. "The superintendent's office is in Greendale Educational Center, just a block or two off the Square."

Joelle nodded. "Great. Thanks, Dad."

"Good luck, honey." Mom kissed the top of Joelle's head on her way out the door. "And remember, keep your cool."

"Yes, Mom." Joelle rolled her eyes.

After her parents were gone, Joelle opened the sports section of the *Greendale Gazette*. It was pretty small. Nothing like the *Minneapolis Tribune*. But she wanted to see how the Twins had done in their preseason game yesterday. She was keeping her eye on Dave Hillmer, a rookie from Georgia. Joelle was sure he'd make it to the majors this season. Jason had said no way. Which only made Joelle want to see it happen even more.

She shoveled cereal into her mouth and scanned past a few articles on the Iowa Hawkeyes, a college team. The Hawkeyes sure were a big deal around here. Fine, but where were the Twins? This newspaper was useless. Another strike against Greendale.

Wait a minute. Joelle sat up a little straighter. The *Trib* never covered middle school baseball, but the neighborhood *Free Press* did. That paper had run several articles on her team last year. Joelle's stats were in them. One had even featured a picture of her.

Joelle had saved every one of those articles. She had stacked them in a neat pile, tied a string around them, and stuck them in a special shoe box. The shoe box hadn't been unpacked yet, but Joelle was pretty sure she knew which carton it was in. If she took that stack of articles with her to the superintendent's office this afternoon, he'd see what a serious ball player she was. And while she was at it, maybe she should grab a few copies of Jason's *Trib* articles from last year, too. That would show the superintendent that good baseball genes ran in the family.

Leaving her breakfast unfinished, Joelle pushed back her chair and raced up the stairs.

* * *

"You're going to do *what?*" Elizabeth asked as the two of them walked to school together.

Joelle switched her clarinet case to her other hand. "I'm going to the superintendent's office after school today and see what I have to do for them to let me play baseball. Want to come with me?"

"I can't. I have softball."

"Oh, right." Joelle glanced sideways at Elizabeth. "Hey, maybe you should think about switching to baseball."

Elizabeth's eyes widened. "Me?"

"Sure, why not? You've got a great arm."

Elizabeth shook her head. "Thanks, Joelle, but no thanks."

Joelle dug into her backpack as she walked until she found her newspaper clippings. "Hey, I want to show you something. At my old school—" But before she could say more, a sudden gust of wind blew one of the articles out of her hands.

"Yikes!" Joelle chased the paper across the grass and into the street. As she reached out to grab it, a cyclist skidded to a stop inches from her hand.

Joelle looked up. Oh *no!* It was the same boy she'd almost collided with earlier when she was out jogging. Rubber Band.

He obviously recognized her, too. "You again?"

Joelle's cheeks burned. "Yeah, me again."

Elizabeth ran out into the street. "Are you okay?"

"She's fine," the boy said. "I didn't hit her." He turned to Joelle. "You sure are a space case," he said, shaking his head.

Space case! Me? "I don't think so." Joelle snatched the clipping and stood up. She was almost the same height as Rubber Band, but she felt a whole lot smaller right now.

"Sure," he said. A breeze riffled through his hair. "Whatever you say." With that, he pushed off on his bike and pedaled away.

"Maybe you should watch where you're going for a change!" Joelle called after him. But he had already turned the corner.

"Did you get your article?" Elizabeth asked as the two of them stepped back onto the sidewalk.

"Yep," Joelle said, holding it up. "So who is that guy, anyway? I keep running into him."

Elizabeth's eyebrows shot up. "You don't know?"

"Hey, give me a break," Joelle said. "I just moved here, remember?"

"He's Ryan Carlyle," Elizabeth replied. "As in Coach Carlyle's son."

Chapter Four

"Hey, Joelle, we missed you at tryouts yesterday." The girl at the locker three doors down looked over and smiled.

Joelle almost didn't recognize her. It was the girl with the bouncy blond ponytail from her gym class. Brooke, she remembered. But today, instead of sweats and a T-shirt, Brooke had on a short black skirt with a trendy black and white blouse. Her hair hung in soft waves around her perfect face.

Everything about the girl screamed POPULAR. So why was she talking to Joelle?

"Um, Joelle, this is Brooke Hartle," Elizabeth said, stepping out from behind Joelle. "Remember? She's co-captain of our softball team."

Softball captain? Brooke didn't look like much of a jock, all dressed up like that.

"Oh, yeah." Joelle nodded as she closed her locker. "You're in my gym class. Hi."

Brooke glanced at Joelle's clarinet case. "Looks like I'll be in band with you, too. That's where you're going next, right?"

Joelle fumbled with her schedule slip. She hadn't had band at all yesterday. Did it meet first period today?

"Yes," Elizabeth answered for her. She turned Joelle around and pointed down the hall. "Band room that way."

"So what happened? You didn't show up at softball try-outs." Brooke fell into step with Joelle and Elizabeth.

"I told you," Joelle said evenly, "I'd rather play baseball."

"She went to talk to Coach Carlyle after school," Elizabeth said.

"Wow." Brooke seemed impressed. "He's tough. What did he say?"

"What do you think he said?" Elizabeth sniffed.

"She can't play," Brooke guessed. "Oh, well. Too bad. So are you going to talk to Ms. Fenner and see if you can still be on our team?"

"No, she's going to talk to the superintendent," Elizabeth told her before Joelle could answer.

"Really." Brooke looked at Joelle with respect. "Well, hey. Good for you. It'd be cool to play baseball!"

"You think so?" Joelle asked. For some reason she wouldn't have expected a girl who looked like Brooke to want to play baseball. But looks could be deceiving. "Want to come with me?" Joelle asked. "You could tell the superintendent you want to play, too." *Maybe if I could find at least one more girl who wanted to play baseball,* Joelle thought, *it would make my case stronger.*

"Hmmm, all those cute guys." Brooke tapped her finger against her chin, pretending to think it over.

Cute guys? Joelle cringed.

"But...sorry, I can't," Brooke went on. "I've got my softball teammates to think about."

Right, Joelle thought. *Fine, you stick with softball.*

Brooke stopped in front of the girls' bathroom. "I need to fix my hair. It's a total mess. Anybody else coming in?"

Joelle squinted. Yep, it looked like three or four hairs over there on the right side were just a teensy bit out of place. *Major crisis time.*

Okay, that was nasty, but Joelle couldn't help it. There was something about this girl that bugged her. She was relieved when Elizabeth spoke up. "No, we'd better get to band early. Joelle has to meet Mr. Corcoran."

"Okay." Brooke looked back over her shoulder. "And remember, Joelle. If the superintendent deal turns out to be a bust, you've got a place on the softball team."

"Great. Thanks." Joelle pasted a smile on her face. She was not going to play softball. Especially not on that girl's team.

Once Brooke had disappeared into the bathroom, Joelle asked Elizabeth, "Is she for real? She doesn't exactly strike me as team captain material."

"Well, you haven't seen her on the softball field," Elizabeth replied. "Brooke's amazing. She can hit just about anything. Plus, she's really good at organizing everyone. She's a perfect team captain."

Whatever, Joelle thought. She didn't care how perfect Brooke was. The girl seemed so...fake. She reminded her of Amber Fitz and Kari Roe, a couple of really popular, snobby girls back in Minneapolis.

Joelle followed Elizabeth into what appeared to be the instrument storage room. There was already a crowd of kids milling around, talking and tuning up.

Elizabeth wedged her way between two baritone players. "We put our stuff over here," she told Joelle, dropping her schoolbooks into a row of cubbies along one wall. Shelves of instruments lined the opposite wall. She grabbed a flute case from one of the top shelves, then walked over to a table in the middle of the room to put her instrument together.

Joelle opened her clarinet case and stuck a reed in her mouth to wet it. Just then, she felt a light tapping of sticks on her head.

She whirled around. Ryan-the-Rubber-Band-Coach's-Son was waving a pair of drumsticks at her.

"Hey, Space Case!"

Not again. Joelle groaned silently and turned her back. Couldn't she get away from this guy?

But Joelle forgot all about Ryan as she and Elizabeth entered the band room. "This place is huge!" Joelle said in awe. It was about twice the size of her old band room back in Minneapolis. And there were lots more kids hanging around, too.

"Band is really big in Greendale," Elizabeth told her. "More than half the school signed up last fall."

"*Half* the school?" Joelle said. "Wow."

"Well, well, this must be our new clarinetist." A large man with huge red cheeks and a tiny nose bustled over to greet Joelle. "I'm Mr. Corcoran, the seventh grade band director." He pumped her hand up and down. "Joelle, right?" She couldn't help staring at Mr. Corcoran's mustache. It seemed to curl and uncurl with every word he spoke.

"Right," Joelle replied.

Just then, from the corner of her eye, she saw Brooke walk in with a bassoon.

Brooke Hartle played the *bassoon?* In Joelle's opinion, the bassoon was not a "popular girl" instrument.

"We're glad to have you with us, Joelle," Mr. Corcoran said, smiling. "I'm afraid I'll have to put you at the end of the clarinet section for now. But our third trimester auditions start next week, so maybe you'll earn a higher chair."

"Oh, that's okay," Joelle assured him. "I'm not that good. Really." No need getting Mr. Corcoran's hopes up that she was super musically talented or anything. Jason had quit band after seventh grade. Joelle figured she probably would, too.

She climbed up to the third row of clarinets, dodging music stands as she made her way to the end. A girl with long brown hair moved over to make room. "Hey, I'm not last chair anymore!" She greeted Joelle with a big grin. "I've played clarinet since fourth grade and I'm always last chair. I don't know why. I'm not that bad. But after auditions you'll probably move up and I'll be last chair again."

"Don't bet on it." Joelle sat down and laid her clarinet across her lap. She fastened her reed to the mouthpiece. "I was second-to-last chair at my old school."

"You were? Cool. I'm Kailey. Kailey Robinson." The girl held out her hand. "Sorry, I know I talk a lot. I'm on the *Echo*—you know, the school paper? If you don't talk to people, you don't find out anything. And then everyone complains the paper is boring. What's your name?"

"Joelle."

"Joelle?" Kailey paused a second. "Hey, you're that girl who tried to get on the baseball team yesterday!"

"News sure travels fast around here," Joelle muttered.

Kailey shrugged. "Hey, it's a small school. If you ask me, they should've let you play. I mean, it's not like our baseball team is that good. You couldn't possibly bring them down any lower. I think the real question is why would you want to play on such a lousy team?"

"Well…" Joelle began. But Kailey didn't give her much chance to speak.

"Our *softball* team's not bad," Kailey went on. "But the baseball team only won, like, one game all season last year."

"One win?" *Was that true?* Joelle wondered. *Yikes.*

A girl in the second row of clarinets turned around. "They didn't even win one," she said.

"You talking about the baseball team?" asked a redheaded boy heading toward the French horn section. "Man, they're such losers!"

"Hey!" A guy in an Iowa Hawkeyes shirt banged the bass drum. "Who are you calling losers?"

"Yeah, we're looking way better this season," Ryan spoke up from one of the snares. He glanced at Joelle, then looked away like he was embarrassed.

"Yeah, but are you looking good enough to actually win a couple of games this year?" the redhead asked.

"I bet they'd win a couple if they let Joelle play," said a tiny blond flute player next to Elizabeth. Joelle thought she recognized the girl from gym class.

The bass drummer snorted. "The last thing we need is a girl on our team! That'd just make things worse."

"What's wrong with having girls on your team?" Joelle asked. No one at her old school in Minneapolis would have ever said such a thing. Not about Joelle Cunningham.

The drummer just rolled his eyes.

To Joelle's relief, Mr. Corcoran came in and tapped his baton on his music stand. Everyone immediately quieted down.

All these guys will be playing a different tune, Joelle thought, *once I'm on their stupid baseball team.*

Chapter Five

It wasn't hard for Joelle to find her way to the educational center after school. She tried Center Street first and got lucky. A sign in front of an old brick building in the middle of the block said Greendale Educational Service Center.

Joelle adjusted her backpack, then pulled the heavy door open and stepped inside. A directory on the wall listed the superintendent's office on the third floor. Joelle plodded up the stairs.

She could tell that this building had once been a school. It had the same old concrete block walls and wooden doors with windows. And that same old school smell.

The stairs ended at the third floor. The superintendent's office was just across the hall. Joelle read the doorplate: *Margaret Holland, Superintendent of Schools.* She could hardly believe her luck. The Greendale superintendent was a woman!

Excellent, Joelle told herself. *A woman will definitely see things my way.*

Joelle opened the door and stepped inside a brightly lit

office. A small, birdlike woman sat at a large desk in the middle of the room. She wore a plain white blouse with a necklace of blue beads.

"May I help you?" she asked Joelle.

"Yes. I'd like to see—" Were you supposed to say Ms. Holland? Or *Superintendent* Holland? Joelle didn't know. "I'd like to see the superintendent," she said finally.

The woman blinked without smiling. "Do you have an appointment?"

Appointment? It hadn't occurred to Joelle to make an appointment. "Um, no," she admitted. "But I'm not in any hurry," she added quickly, noticing the tan couch across from the secretary's desk. "I can wait until she's able to see me." Joelle would wait all afternoon and all night if necessary.

The woman pursed her lips, then picked up the phone. "I'll see when Ms. Holland might be available," she said.

Joelle sat down on the couch. She opened her backpack and pulled out the newspaper articles and stat sheets she'd gathered that morning.

"Margaret? There's a student here to see you." The secretary glanced at Joelle as she held the receiver away from her mouth. "What did you say your name was again?"

"Joelle Cunningham," Joelle said. "I'm here because—"

The secretary shook her head and held up a hand for Joelle to be quiet. "All right, I'll tell her," she said into the phone. She hung up and pointed toward the inner office. "You may go in now," she said.

Joelle bounced up. "Great! Thanks."

Margaret Holland looked about Joelle's grandma's age—a lot older than her parents, but not nursing-home old. Her chin-length, dark hair was streaked with gray. She wore a denim dress with a red scarf that matched the red blush on her cheeks and her red lipstick. She stood up when Joelle entered the room and offered her hand. "Hello. I'm Superintendent Holland," she said with a smile. She seemed like a nice enough lady.

Joelle shook the woman's hand. "Joelle Cunningham."

"Have a seat, Joelle. What can I do for you?"

Joelle sat in the hard-backed wooden chair in front of Superintendent Holland's desk. "Well, I just moved here from Minneapolis," she began, placing her newspaper clippings and stat sheets on the desk. The superintendent glanced at them briefly, then back at Joelle.

Stay cool and be polite, Joelle reminded herself. That was the way to get what she wanted. "I'm a seventh grader at Hoover. I played baseball at my old school, so I wanted to try out for the team here, too. But the coach won't let me."

Superintendent Holland cocked her head. "You mean you moved here too late? You missed the softball tryouts?"

"Not softball. *Baseball*. And no, I didn't miss the tryouts. Those were yesterday. But Coach Carlyle says that if I want to play ball in this district, I have to play softball. Because I'm a girl. He and my principal, Mr. White, both told me it's some kind of district policy."

"Well, Joelle." Superintendent Holland folded her hands on her desk and smiled again. "I'm afraid that *is* the policy. You see, as a district, we're required to spend the same amount of money on the girls' athletic program as we spend on the boys' athletic program."

Right. Joelle nodded. She already knew that.

"That means we sponsor just as many girls' sports as we do boys' sports."

"But what if I want to play a sport that you have for boys, but not for girls?" Joelle asked.

The superintendent shifted in her chair. "Well, there *was* a situation a few years back where a young lady wanted to play football."

"Yes, I heard about her," Joelle said. "Her name was Tracy something. And she got to play, right?"

"Yes, I believe she did. But Greendale doesn't have a girls' football team, you see, so in that case—"

"You don't have a girls' baseball team, either," Joelle pointed out.

"No, but we do have a softball team," Superintendent Holland said, still smiling.

"But baseball and softball aren't the same thing!" Joelle was having a hard time keeping her tone reasonable and polite now.

Superintendent Holland didn't seem to notice. "They're pretty close, aren't they? A player hits the ball and runs around bases."

"There's a lot more to it than that!" Joelle insisted. "You use a different kind of ball and a different bat. The ball comes at you at a totally different angle."

Superintendent Holland didn't seem to be listening. She was looking at Joelle's papers again. "What are all these?" she asked.

Joelle leaned forward eagerly. "Newspaper clippings and stat sheets from last year. I highlighted the column with my stats, see?" She handed Superintendent Holland one of the pages.

"Mmmm," the woman said, looking at the stat sheet over the top of her glasses. "Oh yes. I can see that your numbers are higher than a lot of the others."

Joelle closed her eyes and took a deep breath. Obviously, the superintendent had no idea how to read baseball stats.

"Superintendent Holland, I love baseball," Joelle said finally. "And as you can see, I'm…" She didn't want to brag, but what else could she do? "I'm pretty good. So, please can you talk to Coach Carlyle and ask him to let me try out?"

The superintendent shook her head. "I'm very sorry," she said as she handed Joelle back her stats. "In this district, softball is the girls' alternative to baseball."

Joelle bit back her frustration as she folded the pages and stuffed them into the back pocket of her jeans. So that was the end of that. It couldn't be much clearer.

This whole deal was so unfair! Joelle wished her dad had never gotten his stupid promotion and they'd never moved to Greendale.

* * *

Now what? Joelle asked herself as she trudged home from the education center by herself. She'd already talked to the coach, the principal, and now the superintendent. There was nobody left to go to. She wasn't going to be allowed to play baseball in Greendale.

Period.

Back home, the Blue Jays would have held tryouts this week, too. Joelle wouldn't have had to try out. Since she was already on the team, it would just have been a busy week of warm-ups, practice, and gearing up for the season ahead. But she wasn't in Minneapolis anymore.

Suddenly Joelle stopped short in the middle of the sidewalk. Maybe there was a way she could go back to Minneapolis!

Her brother still lived there. He had his own place. He was eighteen. Maybe she could move in with him!

Mom and Dad probably wouldn't be thrilled at first, but they'd get used to the idea. It wasn't like she wanted to go off and live on her own. She just wanted to move in with her brother. Her *older* brother who was very responsible.

Yes, this could definitely work!

If Jason agreed.

And of course he'd agree. Why wouldn't he?

Joelle ran the rest of the way home, in record time. The sooner she talked to her brother, the better.

Chapter Six

Are you *crazy?*" Joelle's brother was practically yelling at her over the phone.

"No!" Joelle said, switching the receiver to her other ear. She stretched the phone cord further and sat down at the kitchen table. "Mom and Dad think Greendale is such a great place. Everything's fine for them. But I hate it here! I want to come back to Minneapolis and move in with you."

"No, Jojo," Jason said firmly. "Absolutely not."

"But why not? Come on, Jason. I won't get in your way, I promise. I could cook for you. And clean your apartment."

"You?" Jason laughed. "Cook? Clean?"

"Hey, I'm a lot neater than you are," Joelle pointed out. Dad always said Jason's room would qualify their family for federal disaster relief funds.

Jason snorted. "Well, Jojo, that's a real tempting offer, but it would never work."

"Why not?" Joelle tried not to sound whiny as she twisted the phone cord around her finger. Jason hated whiners. So did she, for that matter.

"Well, for starters, Mom and Dad would never go for it.

Plus, I'm not here a lot. And this place is pretty small. I already have three roommates. We don't have room for another one. Not even one who cooks and cleans."

"I could sleep on the couch."

Jason sighed. "Look, Jojo. You can't move in with me. You're just a kid. You have to live with Mom and Dad."

Joelle bit her lip. "I am not a kid. And I don't belong here," she said.

"Oh, come on. Iowa's not that bad, is it?"

"They won't let me play baseball, Jase," Joelle said in a small voice.

There was a pause on the other end of the line. "What do you mean, they won't let you play baseball?"

Joelle told her brother the whole story.

"Huh!" Jason said when she'd finished. "That *is* pretty bad."

Joelle went to the fridge with the phone and pulled out a carton of juice. "So, *now* can I move in with you?"

"There's got to be something you can do to convince them to let you play," Jason said.

"Like what?"

"I don't know. But I've never known my kid sister to give up so easily."

"I'm not giving up," Joelle protested. "I'm just...out of options."

"You *always* have options, Jojo." Jason sounded almost disappointed in her.

"Well, the only one I've come up with is to move in with you," Joelle grumbled as she sat down at the kitchen table again.

"I told you. That's not an option. You need to find a way to let that coach see what you can do. Then he'll probably be begging you to play."

"Carlyle?" Joelle scoffed. "Don't think so."

"Okay, let somebody else see you. Somebody who's in a position to put pressure on the coach."

"Like who?"

"I don't know. Or maybe—" Jason stopped.

"What?" Joelle held her breath.

"How about writing to the newspaper?"

"Jason, what are you talking about?" Joelle said, frowning.

"Look in the paper," Jason told her. "There should be a whole bunch of letters to the editor in the main section."

The *Greendale Gazette* was still on the kitchen table, right where Joelle had left it that morning. She shoved the sports section and the want ads aside. The front-page section was underneath.

Joelle grabbed it and started flipping pages. When she reached one that said "Opinion," she stopped. "Okay," she said slowly. "I think I found it."

There were several letters on the page. One was about some kind of school bond issue. Another was about a local option sales tax, whatever that was. "These all look pretty boring," she told her brother.

"Maybe. But I bet a lot of them talk about letters someone else wrote. Letters in the paper always get noticed. And one from a kid might even get more attention."

"You think so?" Joelle asked doubtfully.

"Sure," Jason answered. "Your civil rights are being violated here. There are bound to be plenty of people out there who'd support you if they knew about the whole girls' baseball deal. Then that coach would have no choice but to let you play."

Joelle took a closer look at the letters. One complimented a Mr. John Sweeney for his "balanced and intelligent" assessment of the school bond issue. But another said Mr. John Sweeney was basically an idiot who didn't understand the issue. Joelle wondered what people would say about a middle school girl who wanted to play baseball.

"Never underestimate the power of the press," Jason said.

Joelle shrugged. It was worth a try. At this point, what did she have to lose? She grabbed a pen from the counter. "Okay, so what should I say?"

"Sorry," Jason said. "No clue."

"Come on, Jason," Joelle urged. "You have to help me out here. I don't know how to write a letter to the editor."

"Well, neither do I. English is my worst subject."

"But you're the one who came up with this bright idea," Joelle pointed out.

"Well…" Jason paused. "Just write about what happened when you went to try out. And why you want to play so badly. Tell people the differences between baseball and softball."

Joelle made a few notes in the margins of the paper.

"Okay, so how do I put all that stuff in a letter?"

"I don't know. You'll have to figure that out," her brother replied. "I've got to go. I'm supposed to be at work already."

"But—"

"Sorry, Joelle," Jason broke in. "I'm serious. I can't be late to work again or I'll get fired. Besides, this is *your* letter, not mine. You have to write it in your own words."

Maybe Jason had a point, Joelle realized. Mr. All-State-Three-Years-in-a-Row had no idea what it felt like to be told he couldn't play ball. But she did. Maybe her words *would* be better.

"Look, hang in there, okay?" Jason said. "Everything'll work out."

"If it doesn't, then can I move in with you?"

Jason laughed. "Later, Jojo."

Joelle glared at him through the phone and hung up. Now that she had a plan of attack, she had to admit she felt a little better.

She didn't even get upset at dinner when she told her parents about her meeting with Superintendent Holland.

"So you're not too disappointed?" Mom raised a questioning eyebrow as she passed the bucket of fried chicken.

Joelle helped herself to a drumstick, then dished up some potato salad. "Well, I was at first," she said truthfully. "But then I called Jason."

"You talked to your brother? How's he doing?"

"He sounded fine."

Mom looked concerned. "I hope he's going to all his classes."

"What do you mean?" Joelle asked. Her brother would never skip any classes.

"Never mind," her mother said.

Dad took a roll from another box. "What did Jason say that put you in such a good mood?"

Joelle told her parents about the letter to the editor idea.

"Hmm, I don't know," Mom said slowly. "That might not be such a good idea."

"Why not?" Joelle asked, putting down the drumstick.

"Well, when you write a letter to the paper, your words are right out there for everyone to see. People will form opinions about you. And some of those opinions may not be entirely positive. Would you be able to handle that?"

Joelle shrugged. "Sure." Anyone who saw her reasons spelled out in black and white would surely agree with her. Not letting girls play baseball was just plain wrong.

"Your mother's got a point, Joelle," Dad said. "There can definitely be consequences to going on record. But that doesn't mean you shouldn't do it. Not if you feel strongly about something."

"Maybe the question is, how strongly do you feel about this, Joelle?" Mom asked. "What do you hope to accomplish by writing to the newspaper?"

Joelle thought for a minute. "I just want people to know what happened to me. Maybe if enough people see my letter, something will happen to change the dumb policy." *And maybe I can still get to play this season*, she added to herself.

Her parents exchanged looks. The fact that they didn't answer right away told Joelle that they were at least considering giving her permission.

"Well, okay. But I want to see that letter before you send it in," Mom said finally.

"Deal!" Joelle grinned. Now she felt a *lot* better.

* * *

After dinner, Joelle went straight to her room to work on her letter. Luckily, she had her own computer, since her parents had upgraded theirs.

It took her a while to figure out exactly what she wanted to say. But she kept at it, adding and deleting and moving words around. Finally she felt satisfied. She read the letter over one more time before she printed it.

Dear Editor:

My name is Joelle Cunningham. I'm 13 and I just moved here from Minneapolis. I've played baseball in Little League and at school ever since I was a little kid. I play first base. People say I'm really good.

But no one will let me play baseball at Hoover Middle School. Coach Carlyle won't even give me a tryout. He says I have to play softball. The principal, Mr. White, told me the same thing. So did Superintendent Holland. As long as there is an alternative sport available, they don't have to let me try out.

How can softball be considered an alternative to baseball? They're not the same sport at all. You use a bigger ball and a bigger bat in softball. Softball pitchers throw underhand. The fields are different, too.

If softball really is the same as baseball, then there's no reason girls shouldn't be allowed to play on the Hoover Hawks. If it isn't the same, then softball isn't really an alternative to baseball.

*I feel like I entered a time warp when I moved here
to Greendale. It was like being transported back to the
1950s. Except in the 1950s, women played baseball for
real. Has anybody ever heard of The All-American
Girls Professional Baseball League?*

> *Sincerely,*
> *Joelle Cunningham*

Even Joelle's parents agreed it was a pretty good letter.

"I think you should delete the names, though," Mom said.

"Why?" Joelle asked. "I told the truth."

"Yes, but it's a lot less confrontational if you don't name names."

"Okay." Joelle sighed. She went back and substituted "my new middle school" for "Hoover Middle School," "the baseball coach" for "Coach Carlyle," "my new principal" for "the principal, Mr. White," and "the superintendent" for "Superintendent Holland." But everyone would know who all those people were. There was only one public middle school in Greendale.

"Now is it okay?" Joelle asked.

Mom reread the letter over her shoulder. "Yes," she said, nodding. "It's very honest and heartfelt."

"Thanks," Joelle said. "So do you think it will make a difference?"

Mom gave Joelle's ponytail a playful tug. "We'll just have to see, won't we?"

Chapter Seven

P sst!" Brooke whispered to Joelle from across the aisle during social studies.

Joelle turned around.

"What did the superintendent say?" Brooke asked, keeping her voice low. Today she was wearing a fringed denim skirt and a gauzy blue blouse. A blue barrette held her hair at the nape of her neck and blue hearts sparkled in her ear lobes. She looked…perfect.

Joelle checked to make sure she wasn't going to get in trouble for talking. But Mr. Hawkings was busy reading.

"She said I couldn't play," Joelle whispered back.

"Bummer." Brooke didn't look too sorry, though. "So you're going to join softball now, right?"

"No."

Brooke frowned. "Why not?"

"I'm just not." Joelle was starting to feel annoyed now. How many times did she have to repeat it?

She tried to get back to her worksheet on courtroom procedure, but Brooke wouldn't shut up. "So what are you saying?"

Brooke asked. "If you can't play baseball, you're not going to play *anything?*" The way she said it made Joelle sound like a spoiled little kid.

"No," Joelle said evenly. "It's just that if I join softball now, people are going to think I was never all that serious about baseball."

"Well, you're not going to be able to play anyway. Everyone's told you that already."

Mr. Hawkings looked up from his reading to see who was talking.

But Joelle wasn't going to let Brooke get the last word. "They might change their minds," she whispered quickly. *If enough people call in and complain after my letter appears in the paper,* she said to herself. *It could happen.*

After school, Joelle went out to the baseball field. Coach Carlyle could keep her off the team for now, but he couldn't stop her from watching practice. She climbed up to the top bleacher behind the fence and took a seat.

The guys were working on bunts. One group was lined up behind home plate. Another was lined up behind third base. As Joelle watched, the guys at home and third bunted, then sprinted to first or second base. Every now and then, one of the boys would glance over in her direction, but nobody said anything to her. Ryan Carlyle seemed to make a special point of ignoring her as he moved up in the line behind home plate.

"Remember, one hand on the bat," Coach Carlyle called as a boy with a buzz cut stepped up to the bag at third. "Find the balance point and everything else will fall into place."

Joelle had done this same exact drill many times. Coach Perry always said that everything he could teach about bunting—grip, bat angle, catching the ball with the bat—happened naturally when you bunted one-handed.

She watched the batter wipe his hand on the back of his sweats, then get into position. He seemed really tense. When the ball came toward him, his hand sort of stuck to the bat and he missed.

The next batter made almost the same mistake. Joelle couldn't hold back. "Drop your hand as soon as the pitcher lets go of the ball!" she called to him.

Several boys turned and glared up at Joelle.

"Who asked you?" the guy with the bat shouted.

"Ignore her," another boy said. "She's not even supposed to be here."

The batter turned back around. This time he did drop his hand as soon as the pitcher released the ball. It popped against the bat and hit the dirt just a couple feet in front of him.

"See?" Joelle muttered as the batter sprinted for first. He didn't look back.

Ryan stepped up to the plate next. The pitcher threw a fastball. Ryan stepped forward, dropped one hand from the bat and nicked the ball down. Perfect. The ball hit the ground to the left of the pitcher and Ryan took off for first base.

"Hustle, hustle!" Coach Carlyle shouted. Joelle wasn't sure whether he was shouting at Ryan or at the pitcher, who was running for the ball. The pitcher threw to first, but Ryan was safe.

"Good play!" Joelle clapped.

Coach Carlyle looked over his shoulder. His eyes narrowed and his whole face had a pinched look. "Excuse me," he said, lumbering over to the fence. "What do you think you're doing?"

"N-nothing," Joelle said. Her heart was pounding. "Just watching."

"You're distracting my players."

"I'm not distracting them," Joelle said. "I'm just sitting here. And trying to offer some helpful advice."

"It would be a lot more helpful if you left," the coach said.

"Aw, let her stay, Coach," yelled one of the guys clustered around home plate. "She could be our team mascot."

"How about bat girl?" another player snickered.

"Oh, you wish!" Joelle shouted, one hand on her hip. *Bat girl!* The way some of these guys were playing, they'd be lucky to qualify to carry bats.

"That's enough, boys, back to work!" Coach Carlyle folded his arms tightly across his chest and focused his attention on the drill. He completely ignored Joelle.

She sat down.

Well, she'd won that one. Or had she?

* * *

For the next few days, Joelle kept trudging out to the baseball field after school to watch the Hawks practice. When the guys did their warm-ups, Joelle did her own stretching behind the fence. A couple of the players looked over and shook their heads when they realized what she was doing. But most of them, like their coach, ignored her.

Once the boys started their drills, Joelle plopped down on the top bleacher to watch. After that first day, she never said a word. She just watched.

It wasn't always easy to keep her mouth shut. But if she didn't actually say anything, Coach Carlyle couldn't complain she was bothering his team. Hey, it was a free country. She could do sit-ups and jumping jacks if she felt like it. And there was no law against watching, right?

At least Coach Carlyle will realize I'm serious about baseball, Joelle told herself. She even went to the Hawks' opening game on Tuesday after school. She couldn't help yelling whenever they struck out or missed the ball. But everyone else in the small crowd was shouting at them, too. It was frustrating to watch the guys make error after error. Hoover lost 2–8.

It must have been frustrating for Coach Carlyle, too. He really laid into his players at the next practice. The boys sat in a straight row along the foul line, heads down, as the coach listed off all the things they'd done wrong. Even though Joelle didn't think Coach Carlyle should yell so much, she had to agree with every point he made. Pay attention. Watch the ball. And *hustle.*

But the whole time, the coach never seemed to notice her.

* * *

"Why do you do this to yourself, Joelle?" Elizabeth asked as she climbed the bleachers to where Joelle was sitting one afternoon. Her gym bag was slung over her shoulder.

Joelle glanced up at her friend, shading her eyes from the bright sun. "Hey, don't you have softball practice?"

"Not today." Elizabeth pulled the elastic band out of her hair and her long red curls tumbled to her shoulders. She sat down next to Joelle. "We don't have practice on Wednesdays."

"Hey, Elizabeth!" a girl's voice called from behind the bleachers. "A bunch of us are going over to Caitlyn's. You want to come?"

"Can Joelle come, too?" Elizabeth called back.

Joelle bit her lip nervously. She recognized the girl from one of her classes, but she didn't really know her.

The girl shrugged. "I guess."

Joelle knew when she wasn't wanted. "Hey, no problem," she told Elizabeth. "I'd rather sit here and watch the guys practice anyway. You go ahead."

"No, that's okay," Elizabeth said. She waved down the girl. "I'll see you tomorrow, Shelby."

After Shelby had left, Elizabeth hugged her knees and looked at Joelle curiously. "Why do you sit here and watch the guys like this all the time?" she asked.

"I don't know," Joelle said glumly. "I guess I'm still hoping for some miracle."

She hadn't told Elizabeth about her letter to the editor. She hadn't told anyone. More than a week had gone by. The *Gazette* probably wasn't even going to print it.

Joelle had no idea what she'd do then.

She looked back down at the field. "You know, my whole life used to be about baseball," she told Elizabeth. "I played. My brother played. My family went to tons of games. Twins games. Minor league games. School games. There was hardly a week during the spring and summer that we weren't at a ball park somewhere."

She stared down at the ground through the bleachers. "But it's different here. My brother's not here. There's no professional ball team here. And now I can't even play, myself. I...I really miss baseball, Elizabeth. I don't know who I am without it. Does that make sense?"

Elizabeth looked away. "Sort of," she said softly. "That's pretty much how I felt when my mom left."

Joelle opened her mouth, but no words came out. She didn't know what to say. "Your mom...*left?*"

Elizabeth nodded. "On Christmas Day last year. With some guy. She just told my dad this wasn't the life she wanted and then she was gone."

"Wow." Joelle felt terrible. Her own problem seemed pretty insignificant in comparison to her friend's. "Do you ever, um, hear from her?"

Elizabeth shrugged. "Sometimes. Not a lot. At first I kept hoping she'd come back, but I don't think she will. I don't really want to talk about it." She blinked away tears.

"Okay, sure," Joelle answered carefully. But she had a feeling Elizabeth probably did need to talk about it. Maybe not right now, especially here in the middle of baseball practice. But sometime.

Joelle cleared her throat. "Um, if you ever do want to talk,

53

let me know, okay?" Joelle wasn't sure she'd be very good at talking or listening. She hadn't had a lot of practice. Most of her friends back in Minneapolis were guys. They didn't sit around and talk much. But Joelle was willing to give it a try.

"Okay." Elizabeth sniffed and quickly swiped her eyes. "I'm fine. Thanks, Joelle."

Joelle knew her friend wasn't fine. But she didn't want to be pushy.

The two of them sat together in silence for a while, watching the Hawks practice fielding.

"Some of these guys are really terrible," Joelle said, resting her chin in her hands.

"Ryan's not so bad," Elizabeth said as Rubber Band jumped up to catch a pop fly. "You know, he asked me about you the other day."

Joelle tucked her hair behind her ear. "Oh yeah? What did he say?" she asked, keeping her gaze on the practice field.

"He just wanted to know who you were," Elizabeth said, shrugging. "I told him your name and that you just moved here from Minneapolis. I think maybe he likes you."

A boy liked her? As in *liked* her liked her? "What makes you think that?"

Elizabeth smiled. "Just a hunch."

Joelle chewed the inside of her cheek and watched Ryan as he jogged back to the end of the line. He *was* kind of cute, she had to admit.

Coach Carlyle blew his whistle. "Okay, that's it for today!" he called.

Most of the Hawks bolted toward the school as though they'd been released from prison. But Ryan stayed behind to help his dad gather equipment. He didn't look up at the bleachers.

Joelle rose to her feet. "I guess we should go, too." She made a point of not looking Ryan's way, either.

The girls climbed down from the stands and walked along the fence. Joelle glanced over her shoulder once and saw Ryan staring after her. She quickly turned around again, her face burning.

Did Ryan Carlyle actually like her?

Well, it didn't matter, Joelle told herself quickly. It would never work. Ryan Carlyle was the enemy's son.

* * *

Joelle never set her alarm on Saturdays. After getting up at six o'clock every school day during the week to run, she figured she deserved a break. But she was so used to waking up at the crack of dawn, it was hard to sleep late.

She stayed in bed till eight-thirty. Then she pulled on one of Jason's old T-shirts and a pair of sweatpants, ran a comb through her hair, and went out for her run. This time she headed down to the park at the end of the block.

It was a nice day, so there were quite a few other joggers out. Joelle followed the path over a small bridge, around a bend, and toward what looked like a baseball diamond. A group of kids were gathered around a couple of benches next to the fence.

Joelle slowed to take a closer look. Some of the kids looked familiar. She was pretty sure she recognized a boy from her English class. And another from her science class. Several in the group held mitts and bats.

Joelle dropped her pace to a walk, her eyes still focused on the group of ballplayers. A large boy with a Twins cap stepped aside and then Joelle saw who was standing behind him: Ryan Carlyle.

Ryan must have noticed her at exactly the same moment. "Hey!" he called, waving.

Was he talking to *her?* Joelle checked behind her.

"Yeah, you!" Ryan said, pointing straight at Joelle. "You want to play? We've got uneven sides."

Joelle could hardly believe her luck. What had Jason said about letting people see what she could do? And who could be better than Coach Carlyle's son?

"Sure!" Joelle answered eagerly and ran toward the group. A couple of the guys exchanged looks, but she didn't care. She'd show them. Even better, she was finally going to get to play some ball!

"Okay, let's see if she's really as good as she thinks." A guy with a serious acne problem punched a fist into his glove and grinned good-naturedly.

A tall, shaggy-haired boy looked at Joelle. "What's your name again?" He had eyebrows that joined together at the bridge of his nose.

"Joelle."

"I'm Ian. You're on their team," he said, jerking his chin

toward the group of guys who were already starting to take the field.

"Okay," Joelle said. "But I don't have my glove with me."

"You can borrow mine." The boy who was in line to bat after Ian tossed his glove to her.

Joelle caught it. "Thanks."

There weren't enough players to cover all the positions, so Joelle wasn't sure where to go.

"You want to play third?" Ryan called to her.

That wasn't her first choice, but it looked like Ryan had already claimed first base for himself.

"Sure," Joelle said. She couldn't afford to be picky right now. At least she was getting to play.

She didn't get much opportunity to show anyone what she could do during the first inning. Whenever the ball came anywhere near her, the guy playing second ran in front of her yelling, "I got it! I got it!"

That really ticked Joelle off. The guy was all elbows and knees. He reminded her of those droids in *Star Wars* that had to unroll themselves before they could attack. Only this guy never got himself unrolled in time to get the ball.

"Hey, excuse me," Joelle said after the third time he lunged in front of her. "I thought I was playing third."

"Well, uh…" The boy just looked at her with a clueless expression on his face.

Joelle glared at him. "You thought I'd miss?"

"Come on, you guys. Let's just play," the pitcher called. When he adjusted his cap, Joelle recognized him as the Hawks pitcher. "Hughes, play your own position," he added. "And you—" he pointed to Joelle and hesitated.

What? Had he forgotten her name already?

"Just catch the ball when it comes to you, okay?" the pitcher finished.

Duh, Joelle thought. "Thanks," she said sarcastically. "I'll try."

Unfortunately, the ball didn't come her way for the rest of that inning.

When it was Joelle's turn at bat, the guys actually moved in for her. That was totally annoying. But if she got the right pitch, they'd regret it.

"Come on, Joelle!" One of her teammates clapped.

"Hey, look. She's a lefty!" the other pitcher said to his teammates when she took her position. But he didn't sound too worried.

Joelle adjusted her footing and her grip. She let the first pitch go by. One strike. She squared up again. All she needed was a high fastball.

And that was exactly what she got.

Crack! The ball sailed over all the outfielders' heads.

Behind her, Joelle heard Ryan give a low whistle under his breath.

The pitcher took off his cap and watched as the ball fell to the ground over by the playground swings.

Joelle grinned as she dropped the bat and started around the bases. Two guys took off after the ball, but there was no doubt she would make it all the way home.

"All right!" Ryan and the rest of her teammates applauded when she crossed the plate.

"Not bad." A guy with glasses slapped her on the back. He sounded totally surprised.

"Thanks," Joelle replied coolly.

As the morning went on, Joelle got three more hits—a single, a double, and another home run. And Hughes even gave her a chance to field now and then. She didn't get every ball that came her way, but she did all right. By the time the game broke up, some of the guys were almost treating her like one of them.

"Too bad she can't play with the Hawks," Joelle heard the guy with the glasses say to Hughes as they gathered up bats, ball, and gloves. "We could use a few power hitters."

Excellent! Joelle thought. She tossed the glove back to the guy who'd lent it to her. "Maybe you should tell your coach that," she said with a glance at Ryan. He was busy zipping up his equipment bag.

"I don't know," another boy said as he wiped his forehead on the bottom of his shirt. "It might be kind of weird having a girl on the team. I mean, what about the locker room?"

Several of the other Hawks snickered and started to pick up their bikes.

"At my old school, I used the girls' locker room," Joelle said, shrugging. "It was no big deal."

"Yeah, but there's a lot of important stuff that goes on in a locker room. Team building stuff," Hughes said. "You'd miss all that."

"Hey, I've hung out with guys all my life," Joelle said. "And I've always been a team player."

"Well, you can hang with us here," Hughes said as he

swung his leg over the back of his bike. "But at school, forget it, okay?"

Joelle just sighed. This was totally hopeless.

"Ready to go, Carlyle?" another boy said over his shoulder.

"I'm heading the other way today," Ryan replied. "Go on without me."

"Okay." His friend shrugged. "Later, then." He pedaled off with the rest of the guys.

Ryan walked his bike over to Joelle. "So do you live around here?" he asked.

Joelle blinked in surprise. "I live on Morgan Road."

Ryan nodded. "We're on Hodges."

Joelle had no idea where Hodges was. But it must have been near Morgan because Ryan started walking his bike beside her.

It was kind of strange, really. Joelle tried to seem casual, but she wasn't sure how to act around Ryan. Was it because Ryan seemed to like her? Or because his dad coached the Hawks?

Either way, she felt totally nervous.

Ryan didn't seem all that comfortable either. *So why is he walking with me, then?* Joelle wondered.

When they walked up the hill toward Morgan Road, Ryan said finally, "Just for the record, I think my dad should let you play."

"Really?" Joelle glanced sideways at him.

"I told him I thought so, too."

"You did?" That was before he had even seen her play.

"Yeah. It didn't do any good, though," Ryan said, kicking at a stick. "My dad's kind of…"

Sexist? Joelle offered silently.

"I don't know...kind of set in his ways, I guess," Ryan went on. "He's really big on rules, too. But I think that deal about girls playing softball and boys playing baseball is stupid."

Joelle raised her eyebrows. "You do?"

Ryan just nodded.

Hmm, Joelle thought. *Ryan Carlyle isn't anything like his dad.*

They stopped at the corner. "I go this way now," Ryan said, pointing toward the other street. He adjusted the visor of his cap and added, "We play ball at the park pretty much every Saturday. You can come next week if you want."

"Okay," Joelle said as Ryan hopped onto his bike and took off. "Thanks."

She just might show up.

Chapter Eight

Joelle was dreading her clarinet audition during study hall on Tuesday. Chair tryouts included both scales and sight-reading, the same as in Minneapolis.

She never minded the sight-reading part. It was the scales that always killed her. Probably because she never practiced. "That was fine, Joelle," Mr. Corcoran said after she played her A-flat scale. "Let's do the chromatic scale now."

Joelle took a big breath, then started to play. The first few notes usually gave her trouble, but today her pinky rolled right over the keys. She continued on up into the middle register, slowing down when she reached the upper range. Her high notes were pretty screechy, but at least she'd hit them. She snuck in another breath, then started back down.

Mr. Corcoran wrote something on his clipboard. "Okay, good," he said when she reached the end.

Good? Joelle wouldn't have gone that far. But Mr. Corcoran was that kind of teacher. He reminded Joelle of her coach back in Minneapolis. Coach Perry made everyone feel good, whether they were decent players or not.

"So, now that you've been here a couple weeks, how are you settling in at Hoover?" Mr. Corcoran asked as Joelle swabbed out her clarinet.

"I'm doing fine, thanks," Joelle told him.

"It's tough coming in during the middle of the year," Mr. Corcoran went on. "But sometimes it helps if you can get involved in extracurricular activities right away."

Joelle just nodded as she jammed the clarinet pieces into her case. That was exactly what she was trying to do. Get involved in an extracurricular activity. *Baseball.*

"Hey, Joelle." Ryan came into the band room with the next group of kids as she was going out. "How'd the audition go?"

"Okay, I guess. I'm not exactly a first-chair player," she said under her breath.

Ryan grinned. "Me neither. Hey, are you coming to our game this afternoon?"

"I thought it was an away game," Joelle said. Did Ryan want her to go?

"Well, yeah, but it's only in Fairmont," Ryan said. "And those guys aren't very good. We might actually win."

"You think you can beat them on their own field?"

Ryan shrugged. "Like I said, they aren't very good."

It used to be that Joelle could get Jason to drive her when she wanted to go somewhere. But her brother wasn't around anymore. And her parents would be at work all afternoon. "Sorry, I don't think I can," Joelle said. "I don't have a ride."

Ryan looked disappointed. "Too bad," he said. "It'll be sort of weird not having you there."

"It will?" Joelle asked.

"Sure. You're always up there in the stands, watching, you know? Everybody sees you, but nobody says anything."

Joelle wasn't sure how to answer that.

"Actually, we're not supposed to talk about you," Ryan went on. "My dad says we should just pretend you're not there."

Joelle shifted her books from one arm to the other. So Coach Carlyle had at least noticed her. "Does your dad ever say anything good about me?"

Ryan thought for a minute. "Well, he did say once that he admired your determination."

Joelle felt a tiny stab of hope. That was *something*, anyway. "But he doesn't admire my determination enough to let me play."

"Not yet," Ryan admitted as Mr. Corcoran waved him into the band room.

Not yet? Joelle thought. Maybe there was hope.

* * *

The next morning, Joelle returned from her run to find her dad reading the *Gazette* at the kitchen table. He looked up with a smile and handed her the folded-back page. "They didn't change a word you wrote," he said.

They'd finally printed her letter! Joelle excitedly scanned the whole thing. "Nope, they didn't," she said. Wow. Her words looked important in print. She turned to her dad. "Do you think this will make a difference? Will it help get the district policy changed?"

"I don't know," her dad said as he rinsed his coffee cup in the sink. "If enough people agree with you and they're vocal about it, maybe."

Joelle didn't see how anyone could not agree with her. It seemed like a sure thing.

When she got to school, she was surprised to find out that a lot of kids had seen her letter. Or at least they'd heard about it.

She could almost feel a group of girls staring at her as she spun the combination on her locker.

"That's the baseball girl," one of them said in a low voice. "The one who wrote that letter in the paper."

Joelle couldn't tell whether the girl had liked her letter or hated it.

"Can you believe she sits in the bleachers and watches the baseball team practice every single day?" another girl said.

"I know!" said a third. "She's so weird!"

Joelle's cheeks burned. *I am not,* she thought as she buried her head in her locker and gathered the books she needed for the morning. *I just want to play baseball. What's so weird about that?*

Kailey, the girl who sat next to her in band, peered around Joelle's locker door. "Hey, she said. "That was an awesome letter you wrote to the *Gazette*. I'm impressed."

Joelle breathed a sigh of relief. At least *somebody* thought it was okay.

"You really should join the *Echo*, Joelle," Kailey added. "We don't have that many good writers. You could write sports articles, features, whatever you want. What do you say?"

Joelle closed her locker. "Thanks a lot, Kailey, but I don't think so."

"Why not?" Kailey fell into step beside her. "You're a great writer. And we have tons of fun. Sometimes the whole staff stays late on Friday nights to put the paper to bed. We order pizza and hang out. It's—"

"Kailey?" Joelle smiled and put up a hand. "I'm sorry, I really am, but I'm just not interested right now."

"Joelle?" a boy behind her said.

She turned to see Ryan standing near another group of lockers. He was scratching his ear, looking nervous. "Uh, can I talk to you for a minute?" he asked.

Something in his voice made Joelle feel nervous, too.

"I'll catch up with you later, okay?" Joelle told Kailey.

"Whatever. See you in band." Kailey shrugged and continued down the hall.

Joelle walked over to Ryan. "Hey, what's up?" she said. "Did you guys win yesterday?"

"No. We lost 2–6."

"Too bad."

"Yeah." Ryan seemed to be looking everywhere except at her. "Listen, I was wondering whether you were planning to watch us practice after school today."

"Sure," Joelle answered. "I guess so." *He really does like me,* she thought.

Ryan scratched his ear again. "I'm not sure that's such a good idea, Joelle."

"What do you mean?" she asked, feeling her face flush.

"Well, my dad's sort of mad about that letter you wrote to the paper. He thinks you made him sound sexist."

So? Joelle thought. *He is sexist.* But she didn't say anything.

"Look, it might be better if…well, if you didn't show up for a couple days," Ryan said. "Give my dad a chance to calm down."

Joelle didn't answer. *She* was the one who'd been wronged here. And now she was supposed to stay away from the baseball field because Coach Carlyle was upset?

"I don't know why you had to go and do something like that, anyway," Ryan muttered. He seemed to be talking to his feet. "Most of the guys thought you were pretty cool on Saturday. But then you had to go and write that dumb letter and—well, maybe you're not much of a team player after all."

"*I'm* not a team player?" Joelle cried, her voice rising. Several kids stared as they passed in the hall. "Wait a minute. First of all, I wrote that letter way before Saturday. It just took the *Gazette* a long time to print it. Second, I'm not actually *on* the team, remember? That's what my whole letter was about!"

Ryan looked at his tennis shoes again. "You made it sound like my dad blew you off just because you're a girl."

Joelle almost burst out laughing. Wasn't that exactly what Coach Carlyle *had* done? "Come on, Ryan. You know as well as I do, your dad doesn't want any girls on his team."

"If you'd just hung on a bit, I might've been able to change his mind," Ryan said. "But you made him look bad and now he never will."

"I didn't make him look bad," Joelle argued. "All I did was

tell the truth. Besides, I don't need you fighting my battles for me." She didn't need *anyone* fighting her battles for her.

Ryan's eyes went cold. "Fine. Work it out yourself, then. But my dad'll never let you play for the Hawks now. You can bet on that." He turned his back on Joelle and quickly disappeared into the crowd of passing students.

Joelle stared after him. *If I get that district policy changed*, she thought, *your dad won't have much choice.*

Ryan Carlyle could bet on that.

* * *

Later that morning, Joelle still couldn't push Ryan's words out of her mind. She was having trouble focusing in social studies class.

"Now that most of you have completed your courtroom procedure packets," Mr. Hawkings was saying, "we'll move to the next phase of our unit, the mock trial."

Some kids looked interested. A few of them groaned.

"We're going to try a case right here in class," the teacher went on. "Each of you will have a role to play. We'll need a prosecuting attorney, a defense attorney, a plaintiff—these terms should be familiar to you if you've completed your packet. Who remembers what a plaintiff is?"

Several hands shot up.

"Travis?"

"The plaintiff is the person who's been wronged."

"Not necessarily." Mr. Hawkings leaned against the chalkboard. "The plaintiff files the lawsuit, but either party can be awarded damages." He began to walk around the room. "Our attorneys will decide which witnesses they need and they'll ask some of you to play those roles," he went on. "We'll have a week or so for the attorneys to build their cases and prepare witnesses. Then we'll have the trial. Those of you who don't have other roles will serve as jurors."

Ryan raised his hand. "Who's going to be the judge?"

"I am, of course," Mr. Hawkings replied with a smile. "Any other questions?"

"What's the trial going to be about?"

"How about whether a girl should be allowed to play baseball?" a kid called out from the back.

"Yeah!" a few other voices chorused.

Joelle slid down in her seat. The last thing she wanted was to be held up as some classroom example.

"No, I've got something else in mind," Mr. Hawkings said. "You all know the story of Goldilocks and the Three Bears." He pulled a large rag doll out from behind his desk and held her up. "Say hello to our defendant, Goldilocks."

"*That's* our trial?" one boy asked.

"Totally lame!" the kid next to him agreed.

"Just listen." Mr. Hawkings leaned the rag doll against a row of books on his desk. "Goldilocks has been accused of burglary, assault, and destruction of property. If convicted, she faces up to twenty years in prison."

"Well, obviously she's guilty," Brooke spoke up. "She broke into the bears' house, stole their food, destroyed a chair, and slept in one of their beds."

"Yeah, lock Goldilocks up!" a guy near the window said.

Joelle turned and frowned at him. "You'd put Goldilocks in jail?"

The guy's black T-shirt was so faded that Joelle couldn't even tell which band's name had been plastered across the front. His feet rested on the empty chair in front of him. "You do the crime, you do the time," he said with a shrug.

"But she's Goldilocks!" Joelle protested. "She's a children's book heroine."

"So? She broke the law!" Brooke insisted.

Joelle sighed. People in this town were so narrow-minded. Goldilocks should go to jail. Joelle shouldn't play baseball. Did they only see things in black and white?

"What would you do if you were lost in the woods for three days, and didn't have anything to eat or drink—" Joelle began.

"I'd knock," Brooke answered. "I wouldn't just barge in."

"What if no one came to the door?"

"I'd wait for someone to come home."

"Well, what if they didn't come home? How long would you wait?" Joelle shot back.

"I'm just saying, there are *rules*," Brooke said. "If people don't follow the rules, then society can't function. Isn't that right, Mr. Hawkings?"

"Oh no." Mr. Hawkings held up his hands. "This is your argument, not mine. But you're both doing great so far. Brooke, maybe you should play the prosecuting attorney. And Joelle, why don't you be our defense lawyer?"

"That's so perfect," Joelle heard someone behind her mutter. "She's just like Goldilocks. She doesn't care about *rules*."

Joelle forced herself not to turn around.

She really, really hated this town!

* * *

After school Joelle headed toward the baseball field as usual.

Ryan had warned her not to come. But part of her wanted to go anyway, just to prove a point. Nobody could keep Joelle Cunningham down.

Nobody.

But before she was halfway to the field, Joelle changed her mind. *Maybe it would be better to lie low for a while,* she told herself. *Let everyone cool down a little. See what happens with my letter.*

It was hard to do, but Joelle finally turned around and walked back past the softball field.

The girls were practicing on the diamond. From a distance, the drills looked pretty similar to baseball drills. Hitting, running, catching. Joelle stopped to watch. But it just wasn't the same. Elizabeth waved when she spotted her. Joelle waved back.

"Hey, Joelle!" Katie called. Katie was a tiny girl from her social studies class who didn't even come up to Joelle's chin. "Are you playing?"

Several other players, including Brooke, quit in the middle of a relay drill and looked curiously at Joelle. Even Ms. Fenner glanced her way.

"No," Joelle called back. "Sorry." She quickly started walking again. Just because she was giving the baseball team a little space didn't mean she was joining the softball team. Besides, she had to start planning Goldilocks's defense.

She had to do *something* to distract herself from baseball.

Joelle forced herself to think. So who should I call for witnesses? And what should I have them say? Maybe Jason would have a few ideas.

She wanted to talk to her brother anyway. She had a lot to tell him. Joelle dialed Jason's number as soon as she got home. When he answered, she said in a rush, "Hey, it's me! Guess what? My letter got printed in the paper today. Everyone's talking about it at school and—"

"Whoa, Jojo! Hang on. I can't really talk right now."

Joelle frowned at the receiver. "What do you mean? We're already talking, aren't we?

"Well, yeah, but I'm on my way out. I've got a date."

A *date?* "But I have to talk to you, Jason," Joelle insisted. "It's not just about my letter. There's something else, too, and it's really important. We're doing this mock trial in social studies and—"

"I'm sorry, Jojo, but I really can't talk. I'll call you later, okay?"

"Sure," Joelle said glumly. But she had a feeling Jason wasn't going to call.

He had his own life now. Wasn't that what her mom had said?

Chapter Nine

"heck out the editorial page today, honey," Joelle's mom told her a few days later.

Joelle fanned her face with her cap, trying to cool down from her morning run. She staggered over to the kitchen table, where the *Gazette* was lying open.

"You got seven responses to your letter," Dad said.

"Really?" Joelle said eagerly. "What do they say?" She rested her elbows on the back of her dad's chair and peered over his shoulder.

"Well, here's someone who thinks you should be allowed to play." Dad pointed to a letter from a Tom Healey.

Joelle quickly read the letter. Mr. Healey basically repeated everything she had said about baseball and softball being two different sports. *Score one for me*, Joelle thought.

"And here's another supporter." Mom called her attention to the next letter.

Dear Editor,

I play on the Hoover Hawks. When Joelle Cunningham first wanted to join the team, I was glad our coach said no. I thought it would be weird to play with a girl. But some of us played with her in the park the other day. She's pretty good. So she should play if she wants to. Maybe she could even help us win a game or two.

Ian Walsh

Wow, Joelle thought. *That took guts.*

"Nice letter," Dad said. "Do you know this boy?"

"Not really." Joelle shook her head. She and Ian had hardly spoken two words to each other on Saturday.

In another letter a woman said she didn't know much about either baseball or softball. "But if a girl wants to play baseball," she wrote, "I'm behind her one hundred and ten percent!

Joelle snorted. "That woman's only supporting me because I want to do something that most girls don't do."

"Well, at least she's behind you," Mom said. "Not every-body is. Read this one."

Dear Editor,

That girl over at Hoover Middle School should quit whining and just play softball like all the other girls. Baseball is not a girls' sport.

Patrick Quigly

"What?" Joelle cried, outraged. "What does he mean, baseball's not a girl's sport?"

Dad chuckled. "Ignore that one, honey. Here's another that was written by somebody on the school board. Let's see what he has to say."

> Dear Editor,
> I understand Ms. Cunningham's desire to play on the Hoover Middle School baseball team. However, she is presenting the issue strictly from her own point of view. The reality is that we have limited funds for the entire sports program. We are required to spend the same amount of money on boys' athletic programs as we do on girls' athletic programs. If we allow girls to play both baseball and softball, then we'd be offering the girls of Greendale more opportunities than we offer our boys.
> Jeff Fitzpatrick
> Greendale School Board Member

"That's so *stupid!*" Joelle exclaimed. "He makes it sound like I'm the one who's being unfair."

"I must say, I'm really surprised by all this brouhaha." Dad shook his head.

"It's a terrible shame, but I do understand what this man is saying," Mom said. "You wouldn't want the school to cut softball entirely and just have a baseball team, would you, Joelle? There are a lot of girls who play softball."

"I never said anything about anyone cutting softball!" Joelle practically exploded. "Maybe there are boys out there who'd rather play softball just like I'd rather play baseball? Why can't they have both softball and baseball and let kids play whichever one they want?"

She picked up the paper and looked at the rest of the letters. The last one was the worst of all.

> *Dear Editor:*
>
> *Here's a message to Joelle Cunningham: You can't play baseball here, so get over it and join the softball team. The two sports aren't that different and we sure could use you. But you probably won't listen because you'd rather sit out the whole season than play softball. What's the matter, Joelle? Do you think you're too good to play softball? Or do you just like all the attention you get being the poor girl who can't play baseball?*
>
> *Brooke Hartle*
> *Hoover Middle School*
> *Softball Co-Captain*

Joelle gave the newspaper an angry shake and threw it back onto the table. "She's got some nerve!"

Dad grinned. "Sounds like Brooke Hartle is every bit as spunky as you are."

Joelle narrowed her eyes. "Do *not* lump me in the same category with that girl."

"I hate to say it, honey." Mom smoothed Joelle's ponytail. "But 'that girl' has a point, too. It doesn't look like you're going to be able to play baseball here in Greendale. So maybe you *should* give softball a try."

Joelle stared at her mother. "You want me to give up? I thought you were on my side."

"I am, Joelle. But it wouldn't really be giving up," Mom said. "You've tried everything else. Would playing softball with the girls really be so terrible? You might make some nice friends."

"And I'm sure you can play Little League this summer," Dad added. "They aren't affiliated with the school system."

"I can't believe it." Joelle sank into a chair. *"You* think I should join softball, too?" Wasn't her father the one who had bought her first bat and glove? The one who had taken her and Jason to the park every night after supper? The one who'd jumped up and down when he heard Jason would be playing ball for the University of Minnesota?

Dad shrugged. "Well, you never know. You might find you actually *like* softball."

Joelle crossed her arms. "Not if *that girl*"—she nodded toward the crumpled newspaper—"is captain of the team."

Dad read Brooke's letter again. "Oh, come on," he said, tossing the paper in Joelle's lap. "She doesn't sound so bad. I think she's issuing you a challenge."

Joelle stood up, letting the newspaper fall to the floor, and stomped out of the kitchen. "I won't give her the satisfaction," she called over her shoulder.

* * *

There was one thing Joelle really appreciated about the guys she knew in Minneapolis. If they had a problem with you, they told you to your face. They didn't issue challenges to you in the newspaper or talk about you behind your back.

Like Brooke and the girls who followed her around all over school were doing right now.

Joelle knew they were talking about her. She could just tell.

Between second and third period, she heard a voice from behind her. "Hey, Joelle!" Elizabeth waved as she caught up with her. "How's it going?"

Joelle hugged her books tighter to her chest. "I feel totally paranoid. Like everybody's staring at me."

Elizabeth grinned. "Well, you are something of a celebrity around here, I guess. Look at it this way. You've hardly been at school a month, but everybody already knows you."

"They don't know *me*," Joelle said. "To them I'm just 'the girl who wants to play baseball' or 'the girl who won't play softball.'"

"True," Elizabeth admitted.

Joelle was starting to wonder if maybe she should just play softball. At least then kids would like her. Life in Greendale would probably be a whole lot easier.

"You know, some people really admire you," Elizabeth said as they continued down the hall.

Joelle raised one eyebrow. "I seriously doubt that," she said.

"No, they do!" Elizabeth insisted. "You're standing up for what you believe in. That's pretty cool. I wish I was more like that."

Joelle wasn't sure what to say. Elizabeth made her sound so brave. *But she's the brave one*, Joelle thought. *It can't be easy for her, dealing with her mom being gone.*

Elizabeth never seemed to whine or complain or feel sorry for herself. Joelle knew Elizabeth had to be sad and angry sometimes, too. But Joelle had never seen her take her feelings out on anybody else.

Sometimes Joelle wished she were more like Elizabeth.

"Some kids think you're right not to join the softball team," Elizabeth went on. "I even heard a couple of the baseball players say this whole thing has been blown way out of proportion."

"Not all of them are saying that." Joelle sighed. Ryan Carlyle sure wasn't. He hadn't spoken to her since their little discussion in the hall.

"Well, those who aren't probably can't stand the idea of having a girl who's better than they are on their team," Elizabeth said lightly.

"Yeah, right," Joelle answered with a smile. "And what do the girls on the softball team say?"

Elizabeth paused. "Do you really want to know?"

"No," Joelle said. "Probably not."

Whatever it was, it couldn't be good.

* * *

On Wednesday a crowd of kids gathered around the big double doors leading to the band room. "The new chair assignments must be posted," Elizabeth told Joelle. She pressed closer to see the bulletin board. "All right! Sixth chair! I moved up!"

"Congratulations," Joelle said. She wasn't in any hurry to see her new chair assignment. It was one thing to sit at the end of a section with only seven clarinets. But now that she was in a band that had twenty-one clarinets, it seemed a whole lot worse.

"I knew it." Kailey's shoulders slumped as she moved away from the door. "Last chair again."

"Bummer," Joelle said. *I guess that means I'm second to last,* she thought. But when she stepped up to the door, she just about dropped to the floor in shock.

Eleventh chair!

Right in the middle—and in the *second* clarinet section rather than the third section. Joelle had never sat that far up before. How had that happened?

"Hey, you!" A baritone player nudged Joelle. "Can the rest of us see the list, too?"

"I can't believe it," Joelle told Elizabeth as they stepped to the side. "Eleventh chair." Maybe she should reconsider quitting band.

"Hi, Elizabeth." Brooke breezed past the two of them, her bassoon case in hand.

Joelle cleared her throat. "Uh, my name's Joelle," she said. "In case you've forgotten."

Brooke whirled around. "Oh, I haven't forgotten," she said sweetly. "I'd just rather say hello to Elizabeth than to you."

Elizabeth looked down at her feet.

"I've *always* said hello to Elizabeth," Brooke went on, smiling. "It just wouldn't be the same saying hello to you."

What? Was that some sort of reference to me liking baseball better than softball? Joelle wondered.

"Yeah, well, talking to you is pretty much always the same," Joelle shot back.

But Brooke was already gone.

* * *

Before the bell rang in social studies, Joelle felt a tap on her shoulder. She turned around.

The frizzy-haired girl sitting behind her said, "Hey, Joelle. I'm Stephanie." She was wearing a colorful tie-dyed shirt and her mouth was full of heavy silver braces. "So tell me," she went on, "why won't you play softball?"

Joelle just stared at her.

"Hey, I'm not trying to bug you or anything," Stephanie added. "I'm just curious."

Joelle hesitated. How should she answer this time? No one seemed to understand her softball-isn't-baseball argument.

"Is it because you think softball is wimpy?" Stephanie asked. "Or do you just like playing with guys better?" She seemed genuinely interested.

"It's nothing like that," Joelle said cautiously.

"Well, what then?"

"I don't know," Joelle said, shifting in her seat uncomfortably. She felt like she was back in Mr. White's office, trying to explain. "I...um...I like the way a baseball feels in my glove. It just fits, you know? And I like the crack of the ball when you get a good hit."

"There's a crack when you hit a softball, too," Stephanie said. "Right?"

"No. I mean yes." Joelle shook her head. "There is, but it's different. I've always played baseball. I don't even own a softball or a softball glove."

"So buy them," Stephanie said, shrugging.

"You don't understand," Joelle said. "It's not really that simple. Not for me, anyway. We're kind of a baseball family. My brother made All-State three years in a row. He has a scholarship to play baseball for the University of Minnesota. If I want to get one, too, then I need to play for my school."

Stephanie still didn't seem convinced. "But aren't there scholarships for softball players, too?" she asked. "You can play softball in college. You can play it professionally, too. It's even an Olympic sport. I saw it on TV."

Joelle drew back. What was this, Twenty Questions? But she had to admit that Stephanie was right about all of those things. "Look, I never said softball wasn't a real sport or a good sport or anything like that," she said. "It's just not *my* sport." *Plus, I can't stand the captain,* Joelle added silently as Brooke slid into the seat across from her.

"Well, okay. Thanks for trying to explain," the girl said. "I was just wondering."

"No problem," Joelle said. "Nice talking to you." She turned around in her seat again, feeling a little awkward. She'd been afraid the girl was going to make fun of her or start arguing.

But she hadn't.

Maybe I am *getting paranoid these days,* Joelle thought.

"So how are our two attorneys doing?" Mr. Hawkings asked after the bell rang. His eyes fixed on Joelle and Brooke. "Have you been putting your cases together?"

"I've got my witnesses already, Mr. Hawkings," Brooke said. She shot Joelle an I'm-so-much-better-than-you look.

Joelle really wanted to beat Brooke in this trial and wipe that smirk off her face. But the truth was, she hadn't talked to anyone yet about being a witness for her.

She'd better get down to business. Fast.

Joelle had already decided not to put Goldilocks on the stand. A defendant didn't have to testify. A prosecuting attorney—especially one like Brooke—could really make a defendant look bad. Joelle decided to concentrate on other witnesses—Goldilocks's teacher, Goldilocks's neighbor, and maybe the Bears' neighbor—to build her case.

Unfortunately, finding kids who were willing to play those roles wasn't easy. When Mr. Hawkings gave them in-class time to work on the case, Joelle discovered that a lot of her class-mates had already said they'd testify for Brooke. And others just plain refused to testify for Joelle.

"Sorry," one girl told her. "I'd rather be on the jury, so I can't be a witness."

"You've got to be kidding," another girl said. She didn't

even know Joelle. But she was obviously a friend of Brooke's.

Was everyone in the whole class friends with Brooke? Was that girl so popular that no one would help Joelle's case? Even though it was a stupid school assignment?

Yikes. Maybe I should try one of the guys, Joelle decided.

The first boy who caught Joelle's eye was Ryan. He was hunched over a book on his desk, his hair hanging over his face. He seemed oblivious to everything that was going on around him.

Joelle swallowed hard. She was still mad at him and he was probably still mad at her, too. But maybe it was time to clear the air.

She marched over and plopped down in the empty seat in front of Ryan. "Hey," she said.

Ryan looked up. "Hey," he said warily.

"Um…" She scratched her head. Unfortunately, she didn't really know what to say to clear the air. Probably she should apologize. But apologize for what? What had she said that was so wrong?

For a long moment, neither of them said anything at all.

Joelle was about to leave when Ryan shoved his book aside and pushed the hair out of his eyes. "Listen, Joelle," he said finally. "I'm sorry about the other day. But I know my dad a lot better than you do. I know how to deal with him, and you—"

Joelle immediately opened her mouth to protest.

"Can I just finish here?" Ryan looked annoyed.

"Sorry," Joelle said sheepishly. She motioned for him to continue.

"My dad's really big on rules. And order. And doing the right thing."

But the right thing is to let me play! Joelle thought.

"He's got a really strong sense of what's right and what's wrong. That's why I really thought he'd come around eventually. But he got mad at me for standing up for you. And then you started dissing him—"

"I did not!"

"You did, too!"

Joelle thought back to what she'd said the other day. She was pretty sure she *had* called Ryan's dad sexist. But that was the truth.

"Hey, I know he can be tough," Ryan said. "But he's still my dad, you know?"

Joelle lowered her eyes. Yeah, she knew. And she wouldn't like it if anyone put either of her parents down. Even if what the person said was true.

"Okay, I'm sorry. I really am. I'll try not to put your dad down anymore," Joelle promised. She hesitated. "So, can you do one thing for me?" she added.

"What?" Ryan asked, sounding a little suspicious.

"Be one of my witnesses for this trial?"

Ryan seemed relieved. "Sure. Who do you want me to be?"

Joelle opened her notebook and scanned her list of possible witnesses, looking for the perfect part for Ryan. He'd be good in just about any of them. "Well, you could be the pastor at

Goldilocks's church. You can tell everyone that she goes to church and Sunday school every week, picks up litter on the side of the road, and volunteers in the soup kitchen.

"Or you could be her elderly next-door neighbor. Goldilocks always rakes leaves and shovels the sidewalk for him and she never enters his house without an invitation."

"Sounds like Goldilocks is a really, really good person." Ryan cracked a smile.

Joelle smiled back. "Yep, she is."

"Any other parts?" Ryan peered at the other possibilities in Joelle's notebook. "How about if I play the doctor who testifies that Goldilocks was weak with hunger, severely dehydrated, and probably not in her right state of mind when she entered the Bears' house? Or the Bears' neighbor, who finds Goldilocks in the woods and takes her to the doctor?"

"The Bears' neighbor is good," Joelle said, nodding. "He'll probably be important because he could be a witness for either side. He's the one who finds Goldilocks, but he also knows the Bears, so he might have to testify about their characters."

"And everyone knows those Bears are evil, right?" Ryan said with a smirk.

"Right." Joelle laughed.

"Well, I don't know," Ryan said seriously. "You're trying to paint Goldilocks as a perfect citizen. And I bet Brooke will do the same thing with the Bears. But the truth is, neither side is totally evil. It's just like in real life. Both sides have a point."

"Yeah, sure," Joelle said. But she wondered: *Was Ryan talking about the trial? Or the whole crazy baseball mess?*

Chapter Ten

The phone was ringing when Joelle arrived home from school on Thursday. She jammed her key into the lock, banged the door open, and lunged for the receiver.

"Jason?" she answered, out of breath. It *had* to be her brother. She hadn't heard from him in a week.

"No," said a girl's uncertain voice. "I'm looking for Joelle Cunningham. Is this the right number?"

"I'm Joelle." It sounded like the girl was around her age. "Who's this?"

"Well, you don't know me. My name's Mandi Burns. I live in Greendale but I don't go to Hoover because I'm home-schooled. Anyway, I've been reading all those letters in the paper."

"Oh." Joelle sat down at the table. "Right."

"I don't normally call people up like this," Mandi said. "But I really like baseball, too. My aunt played for the Colorado Silver Bullets."

Joelle nearly dropped the receiver. The Silver Bullets were an all-female professional baseball team that had been started in the 1990s. "Really?" she said, impressed.

"Well, she only played one season," Mandi replied. "But yeah. She's the one who taught me how to play."

"You mean, you *play* baseball?" Joelle asked. Another girl—finally!

"Just in the summer," Mandi said. "Parks and Rec has a summer league. It's not a big deal, no tryouts or anything. Anyone who wants to can play."

Joelle switched the receiver to her other hand. "So, did other girls play?"

"My friend Leah did. There were a couple of others from our homeschool group, too. But you know what? Parks and Rec put the girls on separate teams, so no one team was stuck with all of us."

"That stinks! Are any of you playing baseball now?" Joelle asked eagerly.

"There's no place to play. I'm dual enrolled, which means even though I do my schoolwork at home, I can still use school resources and participate in after-school activities. My mom wanted me to do softball this year, but I didn't want to. It's not the same, you know?"

Ha! Joelle *did* know.

"But I'd play baseball if I could," Mandi went on. "So would Leah. You should meet her. She's really good. She's short but she's incredibly fast. Last summer she stole more bases than anyone else in the whole league."

"Cool," Joelle said.

"Hey, maybe you'd want to hang out sometime?" Mandi asked hesitantly. "I could bring Leah, too. We could meet at a park and play a little ball."

"That sounds great," Joelle answered. She and Mandi made plans to meet at Center Park on Saturday morning.

"Okay," Mandi said. "See you then."

"See you then," Joelle echoed. "Bye."

As soon as she hung up, she remembered that Saturday mornings were when Ryan and the guys played at the park by her house. She hadn't gone last week since she and Ryan weren't speaking, but she had planned on going this week.

Meeting Mandi and Leah sounded fun, though. And she'd still be playing baseball.

Well, sort of playing.

It was kind of hard to do much with just three people. Joelle decided to invite Elizabeth to join them.

"Hey, I'm not into baseball, remember?" Elizabeth said when Joelle called her. "I'm not even that great at softball."

"You are, too," Joelle insisted. "All you need is some confidence. We're just going to toss a ball around, maybe hit a few. No big deal. It'll be just like what you and your dad and I play in the backyard. *Please?* It would be a lot more fun with four people than three."

Elizabeth sighed. "Okay, okay. I'll go. But don't say I didn't warn you."

Almost as soon as Joelle and Elizabeth arrived at Center Park on Saturday, they spotted two girls talking near the fence.

One was about half a head shorter than Joelle with shoulder-length, light brown hair. She swung a bat in a lazy arc at her feet and chomped on a wad of gum. The other girl was even shorter. Her straight black hair hung just past her shoulders.

Both girls glanced up as Joelle and Elizabeth approached.

"Hey, is one of you Joelle?" the taller girl called.

"I am," Joelle called back. "And this is my friend, Elizabeth."

The girl suddenly reared back and fired a fastball straight toward them.

Joelle jumped, but Elizabeth stuck out her glove. The ball slammed in.

"What do you mean, you're not a baseball player?" Joelle said, grinning at her friend.

Elizabeth shook her head and threw the ball back. "Just luck," she said.

"Not bad." The taller girl nodded her approval when Joelle and Elizabeth reached her. She totally reeked of grape bubblegum. "I'm Mandi. This is Leah." She jerked her thumb toward her friend.

"Hi!" Leah waved.

Joelle stared at Mandi's thumb. She wiggled her own thumb, then looked back at Mandi's. "Hey, tip your thumb back again," she said.

Mandi bent her thumb back at almost a ninety-degree angle.

"Eeew!" Elizabeth made a face. "How do you *do* that?"

Mandi blew a bubble, then sucked it back into her mouth with a pop. "I'm double-jointed," she said proudly.

"Makes for some pretty interesting pitching," Leah added.

"You're a pitcher?" Joelle asked. Mandi hadn't mentioned that when they spoke on the phone.

"Uh huh." Mandi nodded. "Whenever our homeschool

group gets together, I pitch and Leah catches. How about you guys? What do you play?"

"First base," Joelle replied immediately.

Elizabeth looked down at the ground. "I don't really play baseball," she said, scuffing her foot in the dirt. "I play softball. Right field."

Mandi grinned. "Pitcher. Catcher. First base. Right field. Hey, we've almost got half a team right here."

I wish, Joelle thought. "So, do you guys want to hit a few?" she asked.

"Sure," Mandi said. "I brought a batting helmet and stuff."

"Great!" Joelle said. "Let's go."

They all took turns pitching, batting, and fielding.

"You guys are good," Elizabeth told Mandi and Leah.

"So are you," Mandi replied as she rotated from the pitcher's mound to the outfield.

Leah took her place on the pitcher's mound. "Too bad we don't have anyone here from Greendale Academy," she said, throwing the ball to Elizabeth. Elizabeth caught it and threw it back. "I've heard they're all really good."

Joelle picked up the bat and tapped it against home plate. "What's Greendale Academy?" she asked.

"Remember? I told you about them," Elizabeth said from behind the plate. "That's the private school. Their softball team won the state championship last year."

"Oh yeah," Joelle said. Hmm...that gave her an idea. Greendale Academy surely had a baseball team. And a private school would have different rules than the public school, wouldn't they? If she couldn't play baseball at Hoover, maybe she could play at Greendale Academy. *If* she could get her parents to send her to private school, that is.

"Hey, how much does it cost to go to Greendale Academy?" Joelle asked the other girls.

Leah snorted. "About ten thousand dollars a year."

"And that's if you're a day student," Elizabeth put in. "If you board, it's a lot more."

Well, forget that *idea,* Joelle said to herself. Her parents didn't have that kind of money. And she wasn't the type of student who'd win any kind of academic scholarship.

"You ready?" Leah asked as she tossed the ball back and forth between her hands.

Joelle got into position. "Yeah."

Leah pitched a high fastball and Joelle swung hard.

Crack! The ball sailed over Mandi's head, straight toward a girl who was standing near the fence, watching them.

"Heads up!" Mandi shouted.

Instead of ducking, the girl reached up and caught the ball with one bare hand.

Joelle's mouth dropped open. "That's two perfect reflex catches for the day so far," she said to Elizabeth. "Yours and hers."

"Weird," Elizabeth agreed. "But just luck on my part."

"Sorry about that!" Mandi called to the girl. She ran toward the fence, holding out her glove for the ball.

But the girl didn't throw to Mandi. She stepped forward, brought her right arm back and threw to Leah.

"Wow," Elizabeth said in awe as the ball arched over their heads and slammed into Leah's glove.

"That girl can really throw, too," Joelle said.

"That's some arm," Leah called as she took off her glove and massaged her hand.

"Thanks," the girl called back. She pushed her short, shaggy blond hair out of her eyes and began to walk away.

"Hey, wait up!" Joelle shouted, running after the girl. The others were right behind her. "What's your name?"

The girl stopped and gave them a wary look.

"Where did you learn to catch and throw like that?" Leah asked.

The girl wiped her nose with the sleeve of her faded flannel shirt. "I don't know. My dad, I guess," she said, looking toward the road.

"What's your name?" Joelle asked again.

The girl narrowed her eyes. "Who wants to know?"

Joelle was a little taken back. "Uh, I'm Joelle," she said. Then she introduced each of her friends.

"We all like baseball, so we're just hanging out," Mandi explained.

"You could join us if you want," Elizabeth offered.

The girl hesitated. "Yeah?" she said. Joelle knew the girl was interested. She could see it in her eyes.

"We could really use another outfielder," Mandi said.

"But you don't have to stay in the outfield," Leah added quickly. "We rotate after each play."

The girl shrugged. "Okay," she said.

They all walked back to the diamond together.

"So what *is* your name?" Joelle asked.

"Tara."

"Tara what?" Mandi wanted to know.

"Just Tara," the girl said.

"Well, 'Just Tara,'" Mandi said, "I've got an extra glove in my bag over there." She pointed at the equipment bag by the fence. "Help yourself."

"That's okay. I don't need a glove," Tara said.

Didn't need a glove? Joelle frowned. What was she talking about? Everyone needed a glove.

Mandi jogged over to her bag and dug out the glove. "Here you go," she said, tossing it to Tara.

The girl didn't answer. But she put it on.

They all took their positions. Elizabeth stepped up to the plate and adjusted her batting helmet. Mandi squatted behind her and held out her glove. Joelle went into her windup and pitched a low fastball.

Elizabeth swung and missed.

"Strike one," Mandi called, throwing the ball back.

Joelle waited while Elizabeth took a couple of practice swings. Once her friend was back into position, Joelle pitched again. This time she tried a curve ball. But she wasn't very good at curves yet.

Crack! Elizabeth hit a line drive right between Joelle and Tara. She dropped the bat and ran for first base.

Tara retrieved the ball and threw it all the way home. Elizabeth stopped at second base. Then she went to take a turn on the pitcher's mound and Joelle rotated to the outfield.

"Do you want to play catcher now?" Mandi asked Tara.

"Sure." Tara jogged over to home plate.

Tara was an okay catcher. But once she got up to bat, she blew everyone away. She could blast the ball even further than Joelle.

"Wow, you guys," Leah said finally, glancing at her watch. "It's one o'clock already!"

"It is?" Elizabeth asked.

Joelle checked her own watch. "Uh oh. My parents are probably wondering where I am."

"Mine too," Mandi said as she headed in from the pitcher's mound. "But this was really fun, huh?"

Joelle helped Mandi pack up her equipment bag. "Yeah, it was. We should do this again next Saturday."

"How about before that?" Mandi asked. "Like after school sometime this week?"

Elizabeth shook her head. "Can't. I have softball practice."

"Oh yeah, I forgot," Mandi said. She turned to Tara. "You play, too, I bet."

Tara shook her head. "My school doesn't have a softball team."

Elizabeth, Mandi, and Leah all looked confused. "Where do you go to school?" Mandi asked.

"Across town," Tara said, her eyes lowered.

What other school was across town? Joelle wondered. Wasn't there just Hoover and Greendale Academy?

"You go to Metro?" Elizabeth asked, wide-eyed.

Mandi and Leah stared at Tara as though she had suddenly grown an extra head.

"What's Metro?" Joelle asked.

"It's a school for kids who have problems getting along at regular schools," Tara told her.

"Oh." Joelle blinked. She sort of wished she hadn't asked. "Well, we don't care where you go. Do we?" She turned to the other girls.

"No," Elizabeth said quickly.

"Of course not." Mandi smiled a little too big.

Tara raised an eyebrow. "Don't you guys want to know what I did to get sent to Metro?"

Elizabeth bit her lip.

Mandi and Leah looked away.

Joelle didn't want to ruin a good thing here. It was almost as if Tara was challenging them somehow. "You don't have to tell us if you don't want to," she said carefully.

Tara shrugged. "I didn't do anything. Things aren't so great at home, that's all. I'm not actually from Greendale. I'm from Fairmont. I'm living with a foster family here."

"That must be hard," Elizabeth said gently.

"No big deal," Tara said. "My foster family's okay. But I miss my brother."

Joelle nodded. She sure could sympathize with *that*.

"Well, I'd better get going now," Tara said. "Are we doing this again next Saturday or what?"

"I'm in if the rest of you are," Mandi said.

"Me too," Leah added.

"Okay," Joelle agreed. She looked at Elizabeth, who hesitated, then agreed. "It's settled, then. We'll all meet here next Saturday, ten o'clock?"

"Great," Leah said. "Maybe we could even try to find a few more girls who'd want to play."

"Yeah. Like I said before, we've already got half a team right here," Mandi added.

"A whole team would be even better," Joelle said.

"A girls' baseball team? Right," Tara said. "And who would we play?"

"There's always the Hoover boys' team," Mandi said with a grin. "The Hawks, right?" She nudged Joelle.

Joelle had to smile back. She could just imagine Coach Carlyle's reaction to *that*. "Nah," she said. "Not enough of a challenge for us."

Chapter Eleven

Later that afternoon, Joelle couldn't stop thinking about a whole team of girl baseball players. Was that really such a crazy idea?

But like Tara had said, who would they play?

When the Colorado Silver Bullets was formed, there were no other professional women's teams. So who did *they* play? Joelle wondered.

She went into the den, powered up the computer, and logged onto the Internet. The Silver Bullets had to have a web page. Sure enough, they did. Joelle read about the team's history. It looked like they started out playing against men's minor-league, semiprofessional, and college teams.

There were a lot of other interesting baseball links on that site, too, including a page on women's baseball leagues and another one on girls' baseball leagues. Joelle could hardly believe her eyes. In Rhode Island there was a whole league just for girls ages five to eighteen. It was called the Pawtucket Slaterettes Girls Baseball League. Joelle soon found there were leagues in Canada, Japan, and Australia, too.

But definitely not in Greendale.

Joelle sat back and drummed her fingers on the desk. *Well, why not?* she thought. If they could form an all-girls' league in Rhode Island, why couldn't they form one here?

Joelle jumped into action. It was such an amazing idea, she had to call Jason. Right that second.

But as usual, her brother wasn't home. Joelle was getting used to his annoying answering machine by now.

She cleared her throat and tried to make her voice sound older. "Hello, I'm with the U.S. Census Bureau," she said after the beep. "I'm calling to see whether Jason Cunningham is *still alive!* You're never there when I call and you never call me back, either!" Then she rushed on, "Hey, there's a website I want you to check out. It's *www.womenplayingbaseball.com* and it's got a whole bunch of information on baseball leagues for girls. Hey, Jason, do you think I could try to start one here in Greendale? I was—"

Beeeep!

The answering machine had cut her short. Joelle glared at the receiver. "Call me!" she shouted into it. She knew Jason wouldn't hear that part, but it still made her feel better to yell at him.

Joelle hung up the phone and sighed. She couldn't just sit around and wait for her brother to call her back. Maybe Mandi knew something about women's leagues. Her aunt had played in one, right? She pulled the scrap of paper with Mandi's number from her jeans pocket.

"Hey, Joelle," Mandi answered. "I'm really glad you called. Leah and I had fun this morning."

"So did I," Joelle replied. "Listen, I was just on the computer, looking at the Women Playing Baseball website. Did you know that there's a whole baseball league for girls our age in Rhode Island?"

"No. Really?"

"Really. So what would you think about trying to start one around here?"

There was silence on the other line. "Are you serious?" Mandi asked finally.

"You said you'd play baseball if you had a chance, right?"

"Well, yeah. But—"

"But what? They won't let girls play on school baseball teams in this town and they put the girls on separate teams in the summer league. So why not start our own league? That way, *we* can make the rules."

"Joelle, we're kids. None of us has a clue how to do something like that."

"So? Maybe we can find out. I can e-mail the Slaterettes president in Rhode Island and see how they got started."

It was a long shot, Joelle knew. But no more of a long shot than getting on the Hoover Hawks.

"Well, okay," Mandi said slowly. "I guess it's worth a try."

In the background, Joelle heard Mandi's mom calling her to set the table for supper. Joelle quickly said good-bye to Mandi and started typing her e-mail right away.

Dear League President, she wrote. She chewed the inside of her cheek, trying to figure out what to say next. It was almost as hard as her letter to the newspaper. But that had worked out okay, right? *Short and to the point,* Joelle told herself.

Hi! My name is Joelle Cunningham, and I live in Greendale, Iowa. I want to start a girls' baseball league, but I don't know how. How did you get the Slaterettes started? Could my friends and I do something like this by ourselves? We're thirteen.
Please e-mail me back.
Thanks.

By the next morning, Joelle had received a response.

Dear Joelle,
Sure, you can start a baseball league. Ours began about thirty years ago because a nine-year-old girl wanted to play baseball. What you need to do is start talking to people. Get other girls interested. Get their parents interested, too. You'll need coaches, managers, sponsors, and a place to play. Good luck and let us know what happens!

Nancy Powell

* * *

"You want to start a whole new baseball league?" Elizabeth stared at Joelle in disbelief.

It was Sunday afternoon. Elizabeth and her father were cleaning up the lunch dishes while Joelle sat on a bar stool at their kitchen counter.

"Sure. Why not? If they won't let girls play on the boys team, why not start a league that's just for girls?"

"A baseball league that's just for girls?" Mr. Shaw turned to face Joelle. He had on gray sweats and a navy T-shirt that said World's Greatest Dad. "That sounds interesting."

Joelle told the Shaws about the Pawtucket Slaterettes Girls Baseball League and the information she'd found on women's baseball.

"Hmm." Mr. Shaw put his towel on the cabinet. "I wonder if there would be interest in a girls' baseball league here in Greendale."

"I bet there would!" Joelle cried. "If it was really an option. The thing is, most girls just play softball. They don't even think about it. Girls play softball and boys play baseball. But it doesn't have to be that way!"

"Joelle's right." Mr. Shaw turned to Elizabeth. "I bet you never even considered playing baseball until she moved here, did you, honey?"

"Nope," Elizabeth replied. Her back was to them as she wiped the table.

"But you could." Mr. Shaw was beginning to sound excited now. "There are probably other girls around here who'd play if they had a chance." He crossed his arms and thought for a moment. "I wonder what we'd have to do to get started."

"We?" Joelle said eagerly. "You mean, you'd help us?"

"Are you kidding?" Mr. Shaw's eyes were all lit up like a little kid's at Christmas. "Baseball has always been my game. In fact, when Elizabeth was five or six, I coached her T-ball team. Right, honey?" He gave his daughter a nudge with his elbow.

Elizabeth seemed to be wiping the table extra-hard. "Yep," she mumbled, keeping her head down.

"You'd definitely need coaches," Mr. Shaw said. "I could help out there."

"Really?" That morning Joelle's parents had promised to help with the league however they could, but her dad had told her he was too busy right now with his new job to coach.

"That'd be great, Mr. Shaw!" Joelle said. "I talked to a girls' league president in Rhode Island and she said we'd need managers and sponsors, too." Joelle's dad had said *maybe* Bear Foods could sponsor her team.

"You've already talked to a girls' baseball league president?" Mr. Shaw asked. He pulled out the bar stool beside Joelle and sat down.

"Just by e-mail," she said.

Joelle filled him in on the message she'd received from the Slaterettes president. He listened intently to everything she said. Elizabeth went to rinse her sponge in the sink.

"Do you have any of those e-mail addresses?" Mr. Shaw took a pad of paper and pencil from a kitchen drawer.

Joelle shook her head. "Not on me. But I printed them out at home. And I know you can get them from the Women Playing Baseball website."

Mr. Shaw wrote the information down. "Have you talked to your P.E. teacher about any of this?"

"Well, no," Joelle answered. "Actually, I just came up with the idea yesterday." She glanced at Elizabeth. "Besides, I think Ms. Fenner's kind of busy with softball. I doubt she'd have time to help with a baseball league, too."

"You never know," Mr. Shaw said. "Maybe you should talk

to her. Even if she can't help, she might know other people who can. Don't you think so, Elizabeth?"

Elizabeth turned off the water faucet. "What?" she asked. "Oh. Ms. Fenner? Yeah, she'd probably help out."

Joelle frowned. Her friend was acting kind of weird. What was wrong?

"Well, the first order of business is to find out how many girls we might be talking about here," Mr. Shaw said.

"We could set up some sort of meeting for anyone who's interested," Joelle suggested.

Mr. Shaw nodded. "You'd have to do some advertising for that," he said.

Joelle turned to Elizabeth, who seemed to be busily buzzing around the kitchen, putting away stuff in cabinets. "Maybe we could get together with Mandi and Leah and Tara to make some fliers or something," Joelle said.

"Mmm-hmm," Elizabeth replied.

"Well, great. While you girls figure all that out, I think I'll go do some Web surfing." Mr. Shaw grabbed his notepad, kissed the top of Elizabeth's head, and bounded into the den off the kitchen.

"Wow. Your dad's really into this, isn't he?" Joelle said with a smile.

"Yeah. I guess." Elizabeth lowered her eyes as she slid onto the stool beside Joelle.

Joelle stopped smiling. "Elizabeth, what's wrong? Don't you think a girls' league is a good idea?"

Elizabeth shrugged. "Sure. But I told you, Joelle, I'm not a baseball player. Not like you and Mandi and the others."

"But you can play. I've seen you. You're good."

"Not really. But that doesn't matter. You went and got my dad all excited about the idea, so now I pretty much have to play, whether I want to or not. I'll end up making a fool out of myself."

"You will not!" Joelle argued. "Besides, I'm sure there'll be lots of girls who've never even played at all. That's the point. To give everyone a chance to play."

Elizabeth picked up a pencil and doodled in the margins of the newspaper that was lying on the counter.

"You'd *like* baseball if you gave it a chance, Elizabeth. I know you would," Joelle insisted.

"Maybe," Elizabeth said.

"Didn't you have fun at the park yesterday?"

"Well, yeah, but—"

"But what? Look, just wait until the organizational meeting before you decide anything for sure, okay? If you really don't want to play, you don't have to. No hard feelings. Honest."

Elizabeth shook her head. "You never give up, do you, Joelle?"

"Nope," Joelle answered with a grin. "Never!"

"Okay, I'll think about it," Elizabeth said finally. "I'm sure that'll make you and my dad real happy."

* * *

Joelle hustled down to the gym before band. She wanted to catch Ms. Fenner between classes and see what she thought about a girls' baseball league. But there was a substitute teacher in Ms. Fenner's office. Disappointed, Joelle headed across the commons area to the band room.

"Hey, Joelle." Kailey caught up with her along the way. "It's so boring in the third clarinet section now that you've moved up in the world. I sit by Rachel Morris now. She isn't nearly as interesting as you are."

Joelle laughed. "I miss you, too, Kailey."

"Well, I know how we can hang out together more. You can join the *Echo!*"

"Kailey, I already told you—"

"I'd give you really good assignments," Kailey hurried on. "You could even be the sports editor. None of us are into sports much, so nobody really wants that job. But you'd be great!"

For a split second, the idea of writing sports features sounded fun. But then Joelle came to her senses. "Thanks, Kailey, but I can't. I just don't have time right now."

"What do you mean, you don't have time?" Kailey asked as the girls turned a corner. "I heard you're not hanging out at the baseball field anymore. You've got all kinds of time!"

Joelle hesitated. "Well, I'm working on sort of a big project," she said. She looked around to make sure no one was listening, then leaned close to Kailey. "We may try to start a girls' baseball league."

Kailey's eyes widened. "Really?"

"Me and Elizabeth Shaw and a couple of our friends are working on it. We don't know if we'll be able to do it, but we're sure going to try. So that's why I don't have time to write for the paper now."

Kailey looked impressed. "That sounds cool," she said. "Hey, maybe you could write an article about the league for the *Echo!*"

Talk about never giving up, Joelle thought. Kailey was worse than she was!

"No, really," Kailey said as they continued down the hall. "That way you could get the word out to the whole school at once."

Kailey had a point there. Joelle had already written a letter to the Greendale paper. Maybe writing one article for the *Echo* wouldn't be so bad. And if it would help the league...

"All right," she said finally. "But just one article."

* * *

"So I talked to Mandi last night," Joelle told Elizabeth as they sat down together at lunch. "We're all meeting at the library tonight to make fliers."

"Okay." Elizabeth opened her milk and took a swallow.

"Okay? Does that mean you'll come, too?" The way Elizabeth had been talking yesterday, Joelle wasn't sure she would.

"I like the idea of a girls' baseball league," Elizabeth said, shrugging. "And I really like those other girls. So I'm willing to help you and everything. I'm just not sure I really want to play."

"That's good enough for me," Joelle said as she picked the lettuce out of her taco and popped it into her mouth.

Elizabeth would come around. Joelle was sure of it.

107

That night, Joelle and Elizabeth met Mandi, Leah, and Tara at the library as planned. The librarian unlocked one of the small conference rooms for them, and the girls spread out around the oval table.

"I can't believe we're really doing this," Mandi said.

Leah opened the large black book she had brought with her. It was one of those fancy sketchbooks from an art supply store.

"Wow, Leah!" Elizabeth peered over Leah's shoulder. "Did you draw that? It's really good."

Joelle leaned across the table. The girl winding up to pitch on Leah's paper looked so *real*. "Amazing," she agreed. "I didn't know you could draw like that!"

"Well, considering you've known me for about three days, you can't know everything about me already," Leah said, smiling.

"True," Joelle admitted.

Three days? She felt so comfortable with these girls already. It seemed like she'd known them forever. It was almost like hanging out with the guys back in Minneapolis. Only better. She'd never been part of a group of girls before.

Mandi flipped back a page in Leah's sketchbook. "Show them some of the other sketches you did, Leah," she said. "Leah's been working on ideas ever since you called, Joelle."

There was a drawing of a girl's face with a baseball bat below it and another drawing of a girl up at bat. But the best one showed a pitcher going into her windup. A batter, a catcher, and other players watched anxiously from the dugout.

"I think we should use that one on our flier," Tara said.

"I like it, too," Joelle agreed.

"We could scan it into a computer and then shrink it down to leave room for the writing," Mandi said. "What do we want to say?"

Joelle drummed her fingers on the table. "We probably want to put a big headline at the top."

"How about something like, 'Sick of Softball?'" Tara said.

"Wait a minute," Elizabeth broke in. "Lots of girls actually *like* softball, remember?"

Mandi nodded. "Right" she said quickly. "We don't want to insult anyone. Maybe we should just say something really basic, like 'Join the Greendale Girls' Baseball League.'"

"What if girls from other towns around Greendale want to play?" Tara asked.

"Okay, then," Mandi said. "How about the Eastern Iowa Girls' Baseball League?"

"That sounds good," Joelle said. She liked the idea of players from other towns joining them. There probably weren't enough girls in Greendale who'd want to play, anyway.

"And somewhere below that we need to say, 'Coaches, Sponsors, Players, and Parents: Come to an organizational meeting at the Greendale Library downstairs auditorium on April 20 at 7:00,'" Leah said.

"We definitely got the okay to hold a meeting there?" Elizabeth asked.

"Yup," Joelle replied. "I asked this afternoon when I reserved this study room."

"Let's add our names and phone numbers," Mandi said. "In case somebody wants more information."

"Well, we don't have room for too many numbers," Joelle said. "Why don't we just put yours and mine?"

"You could put my dad's name and number, too, since he's going to coach," Elizabeth added.

"Plus, it would be good to list an adult," Joelle said. "It makes us look more serious."

Leah wrote in all the words around her drawing. "Okay, how's this?" she asked.

"Looks great," Joelle said.

"You did a terrific job, Leah!" Elizabeth said.

"So all we have to do is make copies and put them up," Leah said. "My uncle owns the Mail-It Shop down the street. I bet he'd let us make copies for really cheap. Maybe even for free."

"Excellent," Joelle said. She couldn't believe how well things were coming together so far. Would starting a league really be this easy?

Leah and Elizabeth left the library to make copies while Tara, Mandi, and Joelle stayed to look up places to send some of the fliers. They'd decided to do a mailing to every school, church, library, and grocery store in Greendale and every town within a fifty-mile radius. Joelle was also going to write up a short article about what they were doing for the *Echo*. When it was time to go home, each of them took twenty fliers and a list of places to send them or put them up.

"We'll flood half of Iowa with these," Mandi joked.

"We may need to," Joelle said.

By the time she got home, she was beat. Her mom was watching a courtroom drama in the family room. Joelle plopped down on the couch next to her.

Mom massaged Joelle's temples, just like she used to when Joelle was a little kid. "Jason called while you were out," she said.

"He did?" Joelle started to get up.

"Wait a minute, honey," Mom said. "He's not home right now. He said he had a study group at eight."

Joelle groaned. "Of all the times he could have called me back, he picks the one night I'm out! I've only talked to him once since we moved here."

"Well, this is a busy time for Jason. He's got classes, his job at the pizza place, schoolwork, and this semester he's got baseball, too. I think he has practice every day, plus games. And some of those games are pretty far away."

"It's like Jason's not even in the family anymore," Joelle grumbled as she slumped back against the couch.

"Oh, Joelle. Jason will always be part of our family. But he's got his own life now." Mom put her arm around Joelle. "You're pretty busy these days, too, you know. You've got school, new friends, this whole baseball league business…"

"Yeah, but I still have time for my family." Joelle crossed her arms.

"Your brother said he'd try and get down for a weekend soon," her mother said. "And he's going to e-mail you, too."

Joelle went to the den and checked the computer. There

were e-mails from a couple of the guys back home telling her about their season opener in two inches of snow. They'd beaten Minnetonka 9–5. That was good news. Minnetonka was a tough team.

But there were no e-mails from Jason.

Chapter Twelve

Joelle got to school early the next morning to put up her fliers. She posted one in the cafeteria, one on the library door, and another on the bulletin board outside the guidance counselor's office. A small group of kids gathered around as she was taping a flier on the gym door.

"What does it say?" A girl in the back strained to see over the taller kids.

One of the boys in front read aloud, "Join the Eastern Iowa Girls' Baseball League." His voice cracked on the word "league."

"A baseball league just for *girls?*" a boy with a buzz cut snorted. "What is this, a joke?"

"No," Joelle said, holding tight to her stack of fliers. "The Hoover baseball team is just for boys."

As she finished her sentence, she spotted Coach Carlyle coming out of the boys' locker room.

Great, Joelle thought. *I suppose he'll tell me there's some rule against putting up fliers at school, too.*

But he hardly even glanced at the flier on the wall. Or at

her. "Come on, people," he said, ushering everyone down the hall. "Move along. You're blocking traffic."

Joelle quickly moved along with everyone else, relieved that she didn't have to take down her fliers.

When she got to the girls' gym, she found Ms. Fenner doing paperwork in her office.

Ms. Fenner looked up when Joelle knocked. "Hey, Joelle." The coach rolled up the sleeves of her purple warm-up jacket. "What can I do for you?"

"I have something I want you to see." Joelle handed Ms. Fenner a flier.

The coach glanced at it briefly. "Yes, I saw one when I was up in the office." She shook her head. "I have to tell you, Joelle, I really admire your determination. It's no small undertaking, trying to start a whole new league."

"Thanks." Joelle felt herself blush. "I know you're really busy with softball and everything right now. But I was wondering whether you'd be interested in helping out with our league. If we get it going, I mean."

Ms. Fenner leaned back in her chair. "Help out how?"

"Well, any way you want. We're looking for coaches, sponsors, players, a place to play—you name it, we need it!"

"Yes, I'm sure you will," Ms. Fenner said, chuckling. She picked up a pen and tapped it against her desk. "I'd really like to help you, Joelle, but as you pointed out, I am pretty busy with softball at the moment. Right now the team is my top priority."

Joelle's shoulders slumped. She wasn't really surprised. But still… "What about when the season's over?" Joelle asked quickly. "Would you have time to help out then?"

"Maybe," Ms. Fenner replied. "But I'm not sure you're going to need a league this summer. The rec center has a summer program. And I know they let girls play baseball."

"Yeah, but they put all the girls on separate teams. What I want to do is start a whole league just for girls."

Ms. Fenner looked sympathetic. "That's a nice idea, Joelle. But do you think you'll be able to find enough girls to fill an entire league?"

"We might," Joelle said. "If enough people hear about it."

"Well, even if you find players, you'll still need a place to practice and a place to play. Have you thought about that? There are so many recreation and church groups doing baseball and softball leagues during the summer that it's almost impossible to find playing fields for everyone."

"But where there's a will, there's a way, right?" Joelle said, trying to sound cheerful.

Ms. Fenner didn't say anything.

Okay, maybe cheerful isn't the right tone here, Joelle told herself. She looked down at the stack of fliers in her hands. "So does that mean you're not interested?"

"No, not necessarily," Ms. Fenner said. "I love the idea of a girls' baseball league. I'm just saying there are a lot of things you need to think about."

"I know that," Joelle said again. "And we're trying to figure all of them out. That's sort of the point of this organizational meeting. Would you at least come to our meeting, Ms. Fenner?"

Ms. Fenner smiled. "I'll come to your meeting," she replied.

"You will? Great! Thanks!" Joelle turned to leave.

"I sure wish you'd reconsider softball, Joelle," Ms. Fenner said. "I know my girls would still love to have you."

Joelle found *that* hard to believe. She shifted the stack of fliers to her other arm. "Actually, I think some of them are a little mad that I'd rather play baseball."

Ms. Fenner nodded. "Well, yes, some of them are. But I think they'd get over it pretty quick if you joined them. Hey, they like to win!" The coach grinned.

Who doesn't? Joelle thought. But you had to enjoy the game, too. Wasn't that what grown-ups were always trying to tell kids?

"I'll keep that in mind," Joelle told Ms. Fenner.

* * *

"I don't get it." Brooke told Joelle a few days later when she cornered her in the instrument storage room before band. Brooke was holding a copy of the most recent *Echo,* with Joelle's article in it. "You're trying to start a whole *baseball league?* Why?"

Joelle reached around Brooke to grab her clarinet case. "To give girls a chance to play baseball. Read the article," she said.

Brooke followed Joelle into the band room. "Well, okay, how exactly is it going to work? Are you going to have a bunch of all-girl teams play each other?"

"That's the way a league usually works," Joelle said calmly, climbing up to the second row of clarinets. Brooke, dragging her bassoon with her, trailed Joelle.

116

"So, will people have to try out or will you take anyone who wants to play? How many games and practices will there be each week? Where are you going to play?"

Joelle shrugged as she took her seat. "Don't know yet."

"Who's going to sponsor you? The rec center? Have you talked to them? What about a church?"

What was with all the questions? Was Brooke trying to make Joelle feel stupid just because she didn't have all the answers?

"I really don't know." Joelle opened her music folder.

Brooke rested her arm across Joelle's music stand. "Well, it'd have to be a summer league, obviously. You can't work all that stuff out before summer. So I'll make a deal with you. If you sign up for softball now, then I'll sign up for your baseball league this summer."

Joelle stared at Brooke. The girl was kidding, right? Brooke didn't want to play baseball. And Joelle sure didn't want to play softball! Hadn't she made that perfectly clear?

Joelle shifted in her seat. "Look, let me put this in terms you'll understand, okay? Me playing softball would be like you playing the oboe."

"Huh?" Brooke blinked.

"The bassoon and the oboe are a lot alike," Joelle went on. "They're both woodwind instruments, with double reeds. If you can play one, you should be able to play the other, right?"

"No," Brooke said. "They're totally different instruments."

"Right! And baseball and softball are totally different sports!"

Brooke shook her head. "You're impossible, Joelle! I give up."

Good, Joelle thought as Brooke finally took her seat. *It's about time.*

* * *

After school, Joelle took a bus over to Greendale Academy to put up fliers. She'd heard over and over how great their softball team was. Maybe some of the girls would consider playing baseball.

The campus was on the outskirts of town, surrounded by new housing developments. *Fancy* housing developments, Joelle noted as she watched out the window.

The bus stopped in front of the school and Joelle got off. Greendale Academy was a three-story brick building set back among the trees. The front lawn was thick and green. Not a weed in sight. Joelle felt a little funny about walking on such perfect grass, so she walked along the horseshoe drive that led to the main entrance.

When she stepped inside, she wiped her feet. Everything about Greendale Academy seemed fresh and clean, probably thanks to the elderly janitor who was mopping at the other end of the hall. He had his back to Joelle, so he didn't notice her.

There were several people working in the office. Joelle wondered if she should stop and ask permission to put up her fliers. But there were posters and announcements plastered here and there on the wall. What was the harm in hanging up a few more little pieces of paper? She tacked up two on the big bulletin board across from the front doors. Then she wandered

118

down the hall, taping fliers on bathroom doors, next to the library entrance, and above a drinking fountain. There had to be a gym around somewhere. And where there was a gym, there was probably a gym teacher. Maybe she could talk to her about the baseball league.

"Are you looking for somebody?" A tired-looking girl had just emerged from the bathroom behind Joelle. She wore a blue and gold Greendale Academy sweatshirt and shorts. A sweatband plastered her damp curls against her forehead.

"Yeah, I'm looking for your gym teacher," Joelle said.

"Ms. Azline? She's out on the softball field. Go out that door down there." The girl pointed.

"Great. Thanks." Joelle jogged the rest of the way down the hall and pushed open the door.

She found herself at the back of the school. A huge open area stretched all the way to empty farm fields that were ready for planting. A group of kids, boys and girls, were doing sit-ups and stretches in one area. The boys' baseball team was practicing in another. And further on Joelle spotted the girls' softball team.

Nobody paid any attention to Joelle as she headed toward the softball field. She didn't want to disturb the practice, so she sat down on the grass behind the fence and watched. She'd talk to the coach when they finished.

The softball team was working on throwing and catching drills. There were only four girls sitting on the bench. Everyone else was out on the field.

Coach Azline had on a light blue warm-up suit. She was

tall with dark hair that was graying at the sides. She stood at home plate and batted to different players.

"Use both hands to catch, Sonia," Coach Azline called to the right fielder.

Sonia leaped up and caught the ball in her glove. Then she threw the ball to the pitcher.

"And get your elbow up when you throw," the coach said.

Joelle noticed how serious all the girls seemed. No one was talking, not even the players on the bench. Every player seemed to have her eyes and ears on the drill. No wonder they were state champs.

"Again," Coach Azline said to the pitcher.

The pitcher went into her windup and released. The coach slammed the ball right back at the pitcher, who jumped in surprise, but managed to catch it.

"Look alive, Kelsey!" the coach shouted to her.

Kelsey tossed her long blond hair over her shoulder, then got back into position and pitched again. This time, the coach hit a line drive straight to the shortstop, who ran forward and caught it.

"Not bad, Nikki," the coach said, nodding.

The players on the bench rotated in. Nikki was one of four girls who came off. She glanced curiously at Joelle as she sat down.

Joelle got up and moved behind the bench area. "Nice catch," she said.

All four of the girls on the bench turned around. "Who are you?" Nikki asked. She wore her black hair in about a thousand braids, each one held by a small bead at the end.

"You don't go here, do you?" asked the blond girl who sat beside Nikki.

"No." Joelle leaned against the fence. "I'm Joelle Cunningham. I go to Hoover."

"So what are you doing here?" the dark-haired girl on the other side of Nikki asked. She grinned. "Scoping out your competition?"

"No." Joelle shook her head. "I play baseball. A few of us are trying to get a girls' league going. I came over here to see if any of you guys might be interested."

Nikki cocked her head. "How would it work?"

"Just like any other baseball league. Except it would be all girls," Joelle explained. "We'd play with each other and against each other."

"Excuse me," the coach interrupted. "Do I hear talking over there?" Her hands were on her hips and she looked irritated.

All four girls spun back around.

"Why don't you ladies come back out here," Ms. Azline said. "You can pair up for some more throwing and catching practice."

"If you're interested, come to the organizational meeting at the library next Wednesday," Joelle called as the girls took to the field.

None of them looked back.

Joelle glanced at her watch. Four twenty. Practice wouldn't last much longer. When it was over, maybe she could talk to the girls some more. And to Coach Azline, too.

The practice went on much longer than Joelle expected. After throwing and catching drills, the team moved on to running drills. And after running drills there were even more throwing and catching drills.

Every now and then, someone would look over at Joelle or a pair of girls would whisper among themselves, then look at Joelle. Did that mean some of them were interested?

At about ten after five, Coach Azline must have overheard two girls talking. "What's this about a baseball league?" she asked angrily.

Joelle couldn't hear what the girls were telling their coach, but afterward they all looked over at her.

"Keep going," the coach told the girls. She adjusted her cap, then headed toward Joelle. None of the players moved. Their eyes were on their coach.

Uh oh, Joelle thought, scrambling to her feet. *This lady does not look happy.*

"Look, I don't know who you are or what you're doing here," Coach Azline said when she got close to the fence. "But this is a closed practice. I'd appreciate it if you'd leave."

"I-I just wanted to t-talk to you and those girls," Joelle stammered. The whole team was watching her now. "There's a group of us trying to get a girls' baseball league going and—"

"No one here is interested in a baseball league." The coach folded her arms across her chest and glared at Joelle.

Joelle felt stung. How did this lady know whether they were interested not? A few of them *looked* interested.

"My girls are state champions. They don't need any distractions. Now, please be on your way."

"But—" Joelle began again.

"Please!" The coach barked. Then she whirled around and headed back to the field.

She's worse than Coach Carlyle, Joelle thought.

The Greendale Academy team quickly resumed their drill. But Joelle noticed that Nikki looked back at her over her shoulder.

"Wednesday night! Seven o'clock at the Greendale Public Library!" Joelle called.

Then she turned and ran off the field before Coach Azline threw her off.

Chapter Thirteen

All those fliers must be paying off, Joelle told herself a few days later. People were definitely hearing about the Eastern Iowa Girls' Baseball League. More letters about girls' baseball were beginning to show up in the *Gazette* and on the newspaper's website.

Joelle scanned them eagerly each morning. Some of them were good.

> *Hats off to Joelle Cunningham! Why not start an all-girls' baseball league? Let's keep expanding interest in girls' sports!*

Others were not so good.

> *Greendale does not have sufficient resources to support a girls' baseball league. The few ball fields we do have are not in great shape. Several baseball and softball groups already vie for playing time. How can we as a community divide our resources among so many different groups?*

Joelle skimmed over the letters on other topics and looked for another one on baseball. She was particularly interested in a letter signed by a rec center employee.

> *During the past few years, we've noticed fewer girls signing up for our summer athletic programs. No doubt there are girls in the area who will be interested in playing baseball, but it is unlikely there will be enough of them to fill an entire league. And many of those girls might have signed up for one of our programs. If we don't have enough girls to keep our programs going, we may be forced to cancel some of our programming. Then no girls in Greendale will be playing any sports this summer. If Joelle Cunningham is so eager to play baseball, I would urge the school board to change their policy and allow her to play on her school's team. She would also be welcome to play in our summer baseball league. Perhaps Ms. Cunningham would not feel compelled to start her own league if she could play elsewhere.*
>
> *Jeffrey Tibbetts, Director*
> *Greendale Recreation Center*

Joelle liked Mr. Tibbett's "urging" the school board to allow her to play for Hoover. But it didn't look like that was ever going to happen. That was plenty clear to her now.

So now that she'd finally found an alternative, this Mr. Tibbetts was worried about girls not signing up for programs at the Greendale Recreation Center. What about all the girls who lived in those dinky little towns around Greendale that didn't even have rec centers? They had to come all the way to Greendale for sports. Maybe an area baseball league would give them an opportunity to have a team in their own community.

Joelle sighed.

There was always somebody somewhere telling her no.

* * *

"So what are we going to do now?" Joelle asked Elizabeth's dad after dinner. She had brought the newspaper over to the Shaw's house to show them. "I'm not surprised some people were against the idea of me playing on the Hoover team. But now they don't even want me to form a separate girls' league."

Mr. Shaw glanced at Joelle over the top of his glasses. "We're not going to let a few letter writers get us down, are we?" He put the paper down beside him on the couch and Elizabeth picked it up.

"But what if some of these people actually show up at our meeting and make a big stink?" Joelle asked, frowning.

"Oh, I don't think they will," Mr. Shaw said. "What we need to do is to find out how many girls around here want to play baseball. If just a few show up, then those naysayers don't have anything to worry about. We won't have a league. But if a lot of girls want to play, well…then we'll have to deal with some of these questions. Especially about where we're going to play. There is a shortage of playing fields around here. But we can work something out."

"Okay," Joelle said, trying not to sound discouraged.

"Hey, Joelle." Elizabeth looked up from the editorial page. "Look at this. All the letters against you are from men!"

"What?" Joelle grabbed the newspaper from Elizabeth. She hadn't noticed that before. But Elizabeth was right.

Maybe she should write a response to all those guys. At least she could bring up some of the positive points that no one else had mentioned.

As soon as Joelle got home, she went straight to her computer and started typing.

> *Dear Editor,*
>
> *It's me, Joelle Cunningham, again. I am very upset because so many people don't want me to start a baseball league for girls. Why is it so hard for girls to play baseball around here? A lot of people think softball is the girls' alternative to baseball. But softball was never meant to be that. If you look up the history of softball online, you'll see that the first people who played softball were men!*
>
> *There are definitely other girls who want to play baseball in Greendale. I've met them. They played at the rec center last summer, but they were all put on different teams. We think it would be fun to be on the same team and to play other girls. That's why we're trying to start this league.*
>
> *I'm sorry if there aren't enough fields in Greendale. But does that mean it has to be the girls who don't get to play? Can't we build more fields? Can't we do some-*

*thing? We don't want the rec center to lose business.
And we sure don't want any girls not to be able to play
the sport they want. We just want to play our sport,
too. Is that so wrong? If the rec center is worried about
losing girls, maybe they can sponsor our league.*

Sincerely,
Joelle Cunningham

Joelle reread her letter. She'd just thought of that last part, about the rec center sponsoring their league. Brooke was the one who had put the idea in her head. Joelle hadn't paid much attention to Brooke the other day in band when she'd asked whether the rec center was going to sponsor their league. But it was a pretty good point. If the rec center sponsored the Eastern Iowa Girls' Baseball League, they would supply the coaches, the playing fields, the equipment, and the schedules. Plus, they would get the money from people who signed up. Everyone would be happy. Maybe the guy from the rec center would read her letter and realize what a good idea that was.

Joelle thought about showing her parents her letter, but they were out on a bike ride. And what could they possibly object to, anyway?

She transferred the file over to her parents' computer so she could e-mail it to the newspaper. She added a brief note that said, "Please publish this before Wednesday." She wanted the letter to get there before their organizational meeting.

A few minutes later, Joelle was surprised to find a return e-mail from the newspaper. *Wow,* she thought. *That was fast.*

Dear Concerned Citizen,

We're sorry, but we've already published a letter from you within the last 30 days. We cannot publish more than one letter from any writer within a 30-day period.

Linda Monico, Editor

Great, Joelle thought. *A form letter.* And thirty days from now, the organizational meeting would be long past. She needed to tell her side of the story *now.*

Joelle decided to call up Linda Monico and explain the situation. Surely the editor would understand. The phone number for the editorial department was right there on the *Gazette* website. Joelle was surprised when the editor answered the phone herself.

"Hey, Joelle." Ms. Monico talked as if she and Joelle were old friends. "You sure have sparked a lot of debate around town."

"I know," Joelle said. "Um, I was just wondering why I can't write two letters to the paper during the same month."

"Newspaper policy," the editor explained. "We can't publish the same people's opinions all the time. We need to give other folks a chance to be heard."

Joelle sighed. Another policy. She was getting awfully tired of small town policies.

"But this is a whole new thing," she pointed out to the editor. "The last time I wrote about not being able to play baseball in school. This time it's about starting a girls' baseball league."

"I'm sorry, Joelle," Ms. Monico said firmly. "Both letters are on the same subject, from the same person. You can submit the new one to the Reader's Opinion section of our website if you'd like. But we can't use it in the paper."

Well, the website's better than nothing, Joelle decided. But before she hung up, she had another idea.

"Hey, you're always looking for news stories, right? Maybe instead of printing my letter, could someone interview me about the girls' baseball league? You know, do a whole story about it."

Ms. Monico paused for a moment. "Well, I guess I could check with the features editor. Or maybe sports. It might be possible to send a reporter out to cover the organizational meeting and do a follow-up story," she said. "We'll have to see."

In other words, no promises. "Okay, thanks, Ms. Monico," Joelle said. She hung up and went straight to the newspaper's website. She pasted her letter into the form on the site, but it was too long. She had to do it in two pieces. It wasn't as good as a letter in the paper. But at least her opinion was being heard *somewhere.*

Joelle was about to shut down the computer when she noticed her In Box. She'd been so wrapped up in other things that she hadn't even noticed the e-mail from Jason. She immediately clicked on it.

Hey, Pest,

How's it going? Sorry I haven't called you back. Now that baseball's started, I'm pretty busy. The other guys on the team are really good. Most of them are better than me. I got my position, though. First base. We won our first two games and lost last night. The girls' league sounds great. But sorry, I don't know anything about starting one up. Your trial at school sounds interesting. You'll be a good lawyer because you're so good at arguing! Ha! Seriously, I don't know why you keep calling me for advice. You're doing just fine on your own. You don't need me. Later, Jojo!

Jase

Joelle bit her lip. "I'll always need you, Jason," she said softly as she shut down the computer.

* * *

"Okay, people," Mr. Hawkings said at the end of class on Tuesday. "Our trial begins next Monday. I hope you've all been practicing your parts."

Joelle gulped. She'd been so busy thinking about the league, she hadn't had much chance to prepare for the trial.

"Here's how things will work," the teacher went on. "Each lawyer will present an opening statements. Brooke, since you're the prosecuting attorney, you'll go first. After the opening statements, Brooke will present her case and call her witnesses. Joelle, you'll have a chance to cross-examine Brooke's witnesses. Then Brooke, you'll be able to question your witness again if Joelle brought up anything you want to explain. When you're out of witnesses, Joelle will call her witnesses. You'll cross-examine and she'll redirect. When both sides are finished, you'll each make closing statements and then the case will go to the jury. Any questions?"

Nobody raised a hand. The bell rang and kids began stampeding for the door.

"You may as well give up now, Joelle," Brooke said with a smile as they left the classroom. "This is an open-and-shut case. You don't have a chance."

"Don't bet on it!" Joelle told her. She knew Brooke was just pretending to be kidding.

"Yeah, watch out, Brooke," said another girl behind them. "Joelle always has to win. No matter who she hurts along the way."

"Hey!" Joelle spun around. "That is *so* not true!"

"Whatever you say." The girl shrugged and walked off down the hall with Brooke. Brooke turned and waggled her fingers at Joelle.

"I don't hurt people just to get what I want," Joelle muttered, slumping against a locker. "I don't!" The idea that anyone would think that really made her mad.

Then she thought of Elizabeth. Hadn't her friend said right from the start that she didn't want to play baseball? She'd made that totally clear. Yet Joelle had sort of pushed her into it. Was it because she needed Elizabeth's dad to coach?

Joelle squeezed her eyes shut. *Had* she hurt someone to get what she wanted?

Elizabeth seemed into the whole league deal now. But maybe that was all an act. Maybe she still felt like she had no other choice.

"Hey, Joelle!" Kailey came up beside her. "Anything wrong? You look upset."

Joelle looked away. "Kailey, do I seem like the kind of person who doesn't care about other people as long as I get what I want?"

Kailey raised her eyebrows. "No. You seem like the kind of person who doesn't give up. But I don't think you'd ever hurt anyone on purpose. Why?"

Joelle shrugged. "That's what some kids think, I guess."

Kailey waved a hand. "Oh, don't listen to them," she said. "You're doing a good thing with your baseball league, Joelle. Breaking new ground. Creating new opportunities."

"Too bad everyone else doesn't see it that way," Joelle said, sighing.

"They'll come around," Kailey told her. "Wait and see."

That night after supper, Joelle called Elizabeth. "Hi, it's me," she said when her friend answered. "I need to ask you something."

"Sure. What is it?"

Joelle took a deep breath. "Do you really want to play baseball or did you just get dragged into this whole league thing by me and your dad?"

Elizabeth didn't answer.

"Elizabeth?"

"Well, I do like being part of something big like this," Elizabeth said. "I like the other girls. And it's good for me and my dad to have something to do together. Something to focus on besides my mom."

"But?" Joelle prompted. She could tell there was a "but" coming.

"But I'm just not sure about this, Joelle," Elizabeth said. "I play for fun. I don't take it all as seriously as the rest of you do."

So, I am the kind of person who bowls people over? Joelle asked herself. Just like the girl at school said. She'd been totally insensitive to Elizabeth's feelings, acting as if playing baseball was the only thing that mattered.

"I'm sorry," Elizabeth said.

"No, *I'm* sorry," Joelle said. She cleared her throat. "You're my best friend, Elizabeth. I get a little obsessed about stuff sometimes, especially baseball, but I never meant to force you to do something you didn't want to do."

"I know," Elizabeth said. "And I also know that if I really don't want to do something, I need to stand up and say so."

That's true, too, Joelle thought. But she clamped her mouth shut and gave Elizabeth a chance to continue. There was an uneasy silence.

"Well, if you want to play, it'd be great to have you on the team," Joelle said. "But if you don't, I totally understand. And we can still be best friends even if you decide not to play."

That sounded so weird, Joelle realized suddenly. She'd never had a best friend before.

"Okay, Joelle," Elizabeth said. "Thanks."

But after Joelle hung up, she thought: *If Elizabeth decides not to play, will Mr. Shaw still want to coach? Am I a terrible person for wondering that?*

Joelle had meant everything she'd said to her friend. But she really, really hoped Elizabeth decided to play.

It was okay to hope, wasn't it?

Chapter Fourteen

I can't believe it!" Mandi said as a crowd began to gather in the library's basement auditorium on Wednesday night. "There must be almost a hundred people here!"

"It's amazing," Leah breathed.

"Totally," Elizabeth agreed.

Even so, Joelle was feeling nervous.

Very nervous.

"I just hope all these people really *are* interested in our league," Joelle said. "What if they're here to try and stop us?"

"Hey, it's a lot easier to try and stop one girl than it is to stop a whole bunch," Leah said. She stuck out her hand and Mandi put her hand on top of it. Tara reached in and placed her hand over Mandi's. Elizabeth added hers next.

Joelle grinned and put her hand on top. "All for one and one for all!" she said.

"I hate to break up this little party over here," Mr. Shaw said, coming up and ruffling Elizabeth's hair. "But we need to get this meeting started."

Joelle's parents were right behind Mr. Shaw. "Are you ready, Joelle?" Dad gave Joelle's shoulders a squeeze.

"Do you know what you want to say?" Mom asked.

"Me?" Joelle took a step back. "I'm supposed to get up in front of all these people and start talking?"

"This is *your* project," Mr. Shaw said.

Joelle gulped. She had figured this whole thing would just be a matter of sitting around a table and brainstorming ideas with a small group of girls and their parents. She never expected she'd have to get up in front of a crowd and speak.

"We'll go up there with you," Mandi offered. "Won't we?" She turned to the other girls.

Elizabeth shuddered. "As long as I don't have to talk."

"Me neither," Tara added quickly.

"Would you like me to get things started?" Mr. Shaw asked.

Joelle swallowed hard. "No. We're the ones who want to play, so we should do it." Her heart pounding, she turned and walked to the front of the room. Mandi, Leah, Tara, and Elizabeth followed in a straight line and stood in a half circle behind her.

Joelle wasn't sure how to start. Hopefully something would come to her.

She cleared her throat. There wasn't even a microphone. "Hello," she began loudly. How was she supposed to get all these people to quiet down and listen to her?

"My name is—" She could barely hear herself over the crowd.

Finally some guy in the front stuck two fingers in his mouth and let out a shrill whistle. The room immediately went quiet. Everyone turned to Joelle.

She tried again. "My name is Joelle Cunningham." Her voice shook a little. "I just moved here from Minneapolis." *Get to the point*, she reminded herself.

"I played on my school baseball team in Minneapolis, but the district won't let me play baseball here. They said softball is the same thing as baseball. In Greendale, girls play softball and boys play baseball."

Joelle's parents nodded their encouragement from the middle of the front row. Mr. Shaw gave her a thumbs-up. In the back, Joelle noticed Ms. Fenner listening with interest.

"Well, I've tried to tell everyone that those two sports are totally different," Joelle went on. "And I think it's incredibly unfair that they won't let girls play baseball. I've already found four other girls in this town who like baseball, too."

Mandi, Leah, Tara, and Elizabeth smiled nervously at each other.

"Anyway, we were thinking there might be other girls who'd want to form teams. It would be a lot of fun to play with and against each other. And, well, I guess that's why we're here."

Joelle didn't know what else to say.

"I, for one, think a girls' league is a brilliant idea!" said a heavyset man in the back.

"I second that!" said a woman in a navy business suit.

Joelle breathed a sigh of relief.

"Does anybody here know anything about starting up a league?" a woman asked.

Everyone seemed to start talking at once. It didn't sound to Joelle like anyone had any idea where to begin.

Mr. Shaw stepped to the front of the room and motioned for the crowd to quiet down again. "Hello, everyone. I'm Gary Shaw. Joelle is a friend of my daughter's and also our neighbor. I'd really like to see a girls' baseball league here in Greendale. I know you all have a lot of questions. And I sure don't have all the answers. But maybe if we work together, we can figure out how to get this off the ground."

He went on to tell the crowd what he and Joelle had learned on the Internet. Then everyone started asking questions.

One parent wanted to know how they would form the teams. Another wanted to know where they were going to play. A third wanted to know about sponsors.

"Let's take one thing at a time—" Mr. Shaw said.

A man standing in the back of the room stepped forward.

"That's my dad," Leah whispered to Joelle.

"My brother owns the copy shop down the street. He couldn't be here tonight, but he told me that he might sponsor a team," Leah's dad said.

Then another man stood up from a folding chair in the corner. He was tall and thin with curly blond hair and he wore a Chicago Cubs baseball cap. "I'm Dave Horner. I own the bowling alley in Merrill. I know a couple of girls who might want to play. If we can get a whole team together in Merrill, I'd be willing to sponsor it."

Joelle and Mandi exchanged glances. One thing was for sure. There certainly wasn't any lack of interest here.

"Okay, everybody, we're going to put out some sign-up sheets," Mr. Shaw said finally. He tore off two pages from a yellow legal pad and put them on the table at the front of the room. "I've got one for the kids and another for the adults. Any of you girls who want to play, write your name, address, phone number, and age on this sheet of paper. Everyone else, sign up on the other sheet. Let us know how you can help get this league started."

Once people started getting up and moving around, the room seemed to get even more crowded. Joelle and her friends shrank back a little against the side wall while Mr. Shaw and Joelle's parents talked to some grown-ups.

A woman with short brown hair and freckles walked over and introduced herself to Joelle. "Hi, I'm the elementary school P.E. teacher over in Chesterfield. I'd be happy to coach a team."

Ms. Fenner came up, too. An older woman with whitish hair walked beside her, holding on to Ms. Fenner's arm.

"Hello, girls." Ms. Fenner glanced around. "Quite a turnout you've got here."

"Yeah, isn't it great?" Joelle said eagerly.

Ms. Fenner nodded and glanced at the woman beside her. "Girls, I'd like you to meet my mother, Claire Fenner."

The older woman smiled and held out a hand. Elizabeth took it. "Nice to meet you, Mrs. Fenner," she said politely. "I'm Elizabeth Shaw."

"And I'm Joelle." Joelle shook the woman's hand, too.

"I'm so happy to meet you both," the woman said. She spoke very slowly. "I've been following your situation in the newspaper, you know."

"Mom's always been interested in women's baseball," Ms. Fenner put in.

"My older sister played in the All-American Professional Girls Baseball League during the 1940s. Do you girls know about that?" Ms. Fenner's mom asked.

"Sure," Joelle said. "It was started during World War II when all the major league baseball players went off to fight. There's even a movie about it. *A League of Their Own.*"

"That's right." Ms. Fenner's mother seemed pleased. She squeezed Elizabeth's hand. "I'd really like to see your league get off the ground."

"So would I," Ms. Fenner said. "If you still need another coach, girls, I'd be willing to help. I won't be able to do much before summer, though, I'm afraid."

"That's fine," Joelle said. "I'm not sure we'll be ready until then anyway. Thanks, Ms. Fenner."

Ms. Fenner and her mother moved on and someone else tapped Joelle on the shoulder. It was that girl from Greendale Academy. The shortstop with the zillion braids.

"Hey! Nikki, right?" Joelle said in surprise. "I didn't think you'd—I mean, well, I'm glad you came."

Nikki grinned. "I thought I'd check you guys out. See what you've got."

Joelle introduced Nikki to Elizabeth.

"Hey, I remember you," Elizabeth said. "You're the girl who won the KGRN contest last fall."

"What contest?" Joelle asked.

"It was during the World Series," Nikki explained. "The radio station held a baseball trivia contest at the mall. Anyone could be in it."

"And you won?" Joelle was impressed.

"My dad was in that contest, too," Elizabeth said. "He was so embarrassed that he got beaten by a kid!"

Nikki shrugged. "Hey, I know my baseball."

"So, do you want to play with us?" Joelle asked hopefully.

"Definitely," Nikki replied. "But I don't want to just sit around and talk about it. I want to do it!"

"Well, we're working on that," Joelle said.

"Hey, you guys." Mandi, Leah, and Tara joined their group. They had brought two other girls with them. Two girls who looked exactly alike. Joelle had seen them earlier in the crowd.

"This is Paige. And this is Paula," Mandi said, gesturing to each twin in turn. "They played with us in the rec league last summer." Joelle had no idea how Mandi knew which girl was Paige and which was Paula. Both were tall and thin and wore their blond hair turned under at the shoulders.

"Hi," they said. Their voices even sounded alike, but one of the twins seemed a little shy.

"Paige plays center field and Paula plays right field," Mandi added.

Joelle silently counted up the girls in their little circle. "Do you guys realize that technically—I mean, if we have no alternates or anything—we're only one girl short of a team right here?"

"And look around," Leah said. "All these girls want to play, too."

Joelle sucked in her breath. It did seem as if a lot of kids were interested. But was the Eastern Iowa Girls' Baseball League actually going to happen?

* * *

"Okay, we've got thirty-six girls officially signed up," Mr. Shaw said as he looked over the sign-up sheet.

By this time, most of the crowd had gone home. But Joelle, Mandi, Leah, Elizabeth and their parents had lingered around the table at the front of the auditorium.

"Amazing," Joelle's mom said, shaking her head.

"Yeah, but it's still not enough for a whole league," Joelle said glumly, her chin in her hands.

"And look at all the different ages." Mandi pointed to the sign-up sheet. "We can't have six year olds playing with sixteen year olds."

"We'd have to have divisions within the league," Mr. Shaw said.

Joelle bit her lip and studied the sign-up sheet. "We could put the six through nine year olds together. And the ten through thirteen year olds. And then we could have over-fourteen year olds. What does that leave us with?"

"Not enough for even one team in each division." Leah slumped back in her chair. "Do the math."

Mandi groaned. "This is never going to work out."

"I disagree," Mr. Burns said. "Remember, this was just an organizational meeting. And look how many people showed up. I think we've got a real shot at this."

"We've got several sponsor offers," Mr. Wong noted.

"Coaches, too," Mr. Shaw added.

"We just need to keep at it," Joelle's mom said.

"That's right." Mr. Shaw nodded. "We have to get the word out even more."

"How?" Elizabeth asked.

"Well, if each of you thirty-six girls could find just one more girl who wanted to play, we'd easily have enough to start a league," Joelle's dad pointed out.

"I don't know," Leah said slowly. "Even with seventy-two players, there wouldn't be more than one or two teams in each age group. That's not enough for a league. There wouldn't be enough teams to play against each other."

"Maybe we should just concentrate on one age group to start," Mandi's dad suggested.

Mr. Shaw glanced at the sign up sheet on the table. "Looks like most of the girls range in age between ten and fourteen. We could start with just ten to fourteen year olds."

"But what about everyone else?" Joelle asked. She hated the idea of telling anyone they couldn't play. She knew what *that* felt like.

"It's okay to start small," Mr. Shaw said. "Once we've got a couple of teams together who can play, maybe we'll get more interest within the other age groups."

Mandi's dad nodded. "We've got four towns represented. Greendale, Merrill, Chesterfield, and Fairmont. Let's concentrate on recruiting middle school girls from those towns."

"Depending on how many players we want sitting on the bench at one time, we only need a few more girls from Greendale," Leah spoke up. "That shouldn't be too hard."

"But how are we supposed to find girls from Fairmont,

Chesterfield, and Merrill?" Mandi asked. "We don't know any-one there."

"You'll have to get on the phone," Mrs. Burns said. "Call some of these girls who signed up and get *them* to do some talking."

"We can follow up on our flyer mailings to the gym teach-ers, too," Joelle suggested.

"And we need to alert the media," Mr. Shaw put in. "Newspapers, radio stations, TV stations."

"Hey, did anyone see or talk to a reporter from the *Greendale Gazette?*" Joelle asked. "I talked to Linda Monico a few days ago and she said she might send someone to our meeting to do a story about us."

"I didn't talk to any reporter," Mandi said.

"Me neither," Leah put in.

"Darn." Joelle frowned. "I guess she didn't send anyone."

"No problem," Mr. Shaw said. "We'll just call her again and tell her how the meeting went."

Elizabeth, Mandi, Leah, and Joelle divided the sign-up sheet into four parts. Each promised to call nine of the girls who'd signed up and see if they could find just one or two more players who might be interested.

It was a start, anyway.

Joelle began feeling hopeful again as they all headed home. It was definitely possible that their league would get off the ground.

Anything was possible.

She just had to keep believing that.

Chapter Fifteen

Joelle was just stepping out of the shower after gym class when she heard someone say, "But you *have* to come!"

Brooke. Joelle would recognize that snobby voice anywhere.

The other person answered, but her voice was just a mumble. It sounded like Elizabeth, but Joelle couldn't be sure.

Joelle toweled off her hair. She wasn't exactly eavesdropping, but she couldn't help overhearing Brooke's part of the conversation.

"Oh, come on," Brooke was saying. "It's not like you're a real team yet. What's the big deal if you miss one little meeting?"

There was no doubt about it. Brooke was talking to Elizabeth about their baseball meeting tomorrow morning! That made Joelle so mad. Elizabeth didn't need any pressure from Joelle to play baseball. But she didn't need any pressure from Brooke *not* to play, either.

Pulling her towel tighter around her, Joelle stormed over to the lockers. Water dripped from her hair and landed on her bare shoulders.

Brooke and Elizabeth both jumped when they saw Joelle. A couple of the other girls who were getting dressed in that area stepped back out of the way.

"What are you guys talking about?" Joelle asked, glancing from Brooke to Elizabeth.

"Nothing." Elizabeth grabbed a pair of socks from her locker and sat down on the bench without looking at Joelle.

Brooke stood up a little straighter. "We're playing Greendale Academy next week. They're a tough team, so I want to have an extra practice tomorrow morning. But apparently Elizabeth has other plans."

Joelle set her shampoo down on the bench. "Tomorrow's Saturday. You can't schedule an extra practice on a Saturday and expect everyone to show up," she said. It didn't matter that she herself had shown up for plenty of Saturday practices when she played for the Blue Jays in Minneapolis. And she probably would have grumbled about any Blue Jay who didn't show up. But that wasn't the point.

"Joelle," Elizabeth said in a this-is-between-me-and-Brooke tone of voice. But Joelle wasn't about to let Brooke walk all over her friend.

Brooke slammed her locker door closed. "Hey, it's up to you," she told Elizabeth. "Just get your priorities straight, okay?" She quickly gathered up her gym bag and left the locker room.

All the other girls glared at Joelle and Elizabeth, then followed Brooke. Elizabeth stared at the floor.

Joelle sat down on the bench next to Elizabeth. "Are they

giving you a hard time about playing baseball?" Elizabeth hadn't even committed to the girls' league yet.

Elizabeth shrugged. "I can handle it."

What should I do? Joelle wondered. *Tell Elizabeth to skip our meeting and go to softball practice? Yell at Brooke some more?*

"Look, don't worry about it," Elizabeth said. "It's my problem, okay?"

Joelle bit her lip. Elizabeth was right. She had to stay out of this. She knew she was acting pushy again. And it really wasn't any of her business. "Okay," Joelle said. "Whatever you decide. Like Brooke said, it's totally up to you."

But she sure hoped Elizabeth chose baseball.

* * *

"So, how did everybody's phone calls go? Were people still interested in the league?" Joelle asked as the girls gathered around the swings at Center Park the next morning.

She glanced around the group. Elizabeth was sitting in one of the swings, twisting the chains around and around. She really had skipped her softball practice to be here today.

A true friend, Joelle thought.

"This one girl from Merrill said most of her softball team was interested," Leah spoke up.

"Great," Joelle said, nodding. She sat down cross-legged on the grass next to Nikki.

"Yeah, but none of them wants to start until summer," Leah

went on. "They all think it would be too hard to do two sports at once."

"A girl in Fairmont said they already have nine players. They just need a couple of alternates and they'll have a whole team," one of the twins put in. Joelle wasn't sure whether she was Paige or Paula.

"That's great!" Nikki said.

"We don't need many more girls here in Greendale, either," Elizabeth pointed out.

"I guess our next step is finding a place to play," Tara said.

"Why can't we just keep playing here?" Joelle asked. "It's a public park. We're part of the public, right?"

"Sure," Mandi agreed. The other girls nodded.

"We also need a team name," Joelle said.

"It's got to be something that fits us all," Mandi said thoughtfully.

"Well, we all come from Greendale," Leah said.

"A lot of teams have animal names," Elizabeth said. "What are some animals that start with *G?*"

"Gorilla, gecko, giraffe, goat, goose..." The more talkative twin counted them off on her fingers.

Tara scrunched up her nose. "The Greendale *Geese?*"

Everyone laughed.

"Uh, I don't think so." Mandi shook her head. "But Greendale Geckos has a nice ring to it."

"Yeah, but what *is* a gecko?" Tara wanted to know.

"I think it's a lizard," Nikki said.

"A *lizard!*" Leah shrieked.

The group laughed even harder this time.

"How about the Greendale Green Sox?" Elizabeth spoke up.

"Not bad," said Joelle. "It sounds like a real baseball team. Anybody else have any nominations?"

"It does sound like a real team name," Mandi said. "Like a professional team."

"Except it's not," Leah put in.

"I know," Mandi said. "That's why I like it."

"Well then, everyone in favor of Green Sox say 'aye,'" Joelle said.

"Aye!" all the girls except Tara and Paula chorused.

"I liked Geckos," Paula said timidly. "That was unique."

"Socks are kind of lame," Tara said.

"Oh yeah?" Nikki said. "Do you think the Red Sox are lame? Or the White Sox?"

"Well, the White Sox *are* pretty lame," Tara said. "But that's sort of beside the point."

Nikki frowned. "Do you have any better ideas, then?"

"No," Tara said. "I guess not."

"Majority rules," Nikki said.

"All right," Paula sighed.

Tara shrugged. "Fine, you guys win," she said. "We'll be smelly green socks."

"Don't worry," Mandi said with a grin. "We won't stink, I promise."

All of the other Green Sox giggled.

"Great," Joelle said. "So far we've got a name, a coach, and a sponsor. All we need now is one more player. Then we'll have ourselves an actual team!"

* * *

"Hi there, Joelle!" Mr. Shaw called cheerfully over the fence on Sunday afternoon.

Joelle looked up from her notes. It was too nice a day to be cooped up inside, so she was practicing her opening statement for Goldilocks's trial out on the deck.

"I just got off the phone with Kathleen Kennedy," Mr. Shaw said. Elizabeth was standing beside him, sort of bouncing from foot to foot.

Joelle set her notes down and went over to the fence. "Who's that?" she asked.

"A softball coach in Chesterfield." Elizabeth's dad was beaming. "And she just got a whole baseball team together. Eleven players."

Joelle felt a stab of jealousy in her chest. "That puny little town got a whole team together already?" Chesterfield was even smaller than Greendale.

"Hey, if they can find eleven players there, we ought to be able to find a lot more here in Greendale," Elizabeth said. She looked almost as excited as her dad.

"You'd think so," Joelle said. The Green Sox had been making tons of phone calls and posting fliers. But they still didn't have a full team.

"Well, these Chesterfield girls are pretty anxious to play," Mr. Shaw said. "They're holding their first practice Saturday.

So I thought maybe we should start practicing next Saturday, too."

Joelle perked up. "Really?"

Mr. Shaw shrugged. "I don't see why not. It won't be anything too tough, since a couple of the girls still have softball. Maybe a practice or two each week. Wednesdays and Saturdays."

"Sounds great!" Joelle said. "Let's do it."

She couldn't wait to play baseball again.

* * *

"This court is now in session." Mr. Hawkings banged a gavel on his podium at the front of the room. "The Honorable Judge Hawkings is presiding."

Several kids snickered.

The room was arranged so that Brooke and Joelle's chairs were out in front. The six jurors' chairs were off to the side.

"Are the attorneys ready to give their opening statements?" Judge Hawkings asked.

"I am," Brooke replied. She was dressed for the part, in a navy blue shirtdress that made her look a lot older.

Probably her mom's, Joelle told herself.

"Me too, Your Honor," Joelle said. Maybe she shouldn't have worn her regular jeans and T-shirt. Brooke looked a lot more...professional than she did.

Brooke stood up. "Your Honor, distinguished guests, and members of the jury, I will prove that Goldilocks is guilty of the crimes of assault, burglary, and destruction of property. She broke into the Bears' house. She assaulted Papa Bear, stole their food, and broke their brand new chair. We recommend Goldilocks be punished to the full extent of the law."

Joelle got up and rolled her eyes dramatically the way she'd seen lawyers do on TV. "Your Honor, distinguished guests and members of the jury. Goldilocks is not the evil person the prosecution is making her out to be. She's an honor student and community volunteer. She found herself lost in the woods for three days with no food and no water. She came upon a little house, knocked on the door and found nobody home. So she went inside. While she was inside, she ate some food. She accidentally broke a chair. And she did hit Papa Bear, but it was in self-defense. This whole thing has been blown way out of proportion. Goldilocks is a good person and she should be set free."

Brooke called her first witness. Jake Trembley stood up. He was dressed as a hunter in camouflage.

"I warned Goldilocks not to go into the woods," Jake told the court. "But she wouldn't listen. She went in anyway."

"Thank you, Mr. Trembley," Brooke said.

"Had you ever met Goldilocks before?" Joelle asked Jake on cross-examination.

"No."

"Then why should Goldilocks listen to you, a complete stranger? She could have gone into the woods just to get away from you because she wasn't supposed to talk to strangers. Maybe that's why she got lost."

Jake didn't know what to say to that. Joelle felt proud of herself for thinking on her feet.

Danielle, the girl who sat behind Brooke, played Mama Bear. She wore a headband with furry ears attached. Brooke walked her through her story about how the porridge was too hot, so the family decided to take a walk.

Then Joelle stood up.

"So Mama Bear, you claim that Goldilocks broke into your home. Isn't it true that the door was left unlocked?"

"Well, yes, but we were only gone for a few minutes," Danielle answered.

"How can you call it 'breaking in' if the door was unlocked?"

Danielle's eyes darted from Joelle to Brooke. She didn't have an answer.

Another point for my side, Joelle thought as she moved on. "Now, you're a mother bear. That means you're a good and kindhearted soul, correct?"

"Yes." Danielle eyed Joelle warily.

"Well, if you'd been home when Goldilocks arrived at your door, hungry and thirsty and scared and confused, would you have invited her in?"

"I don't know. Maybe."

"And would you have given her some porridge? Asked her to sit down? Maybe even let her take a nap in Baby Bear's bed?"

Danielle looked mad. "Well, I *wasn't* home. And Goldilocks assaulted my husband!" she said.

Several of the "witnesses" behind Joelle laughed.

"Order in the court!" Judge Hawkings banged his gavel.

Joelle raised an eyebrow. "Isn't it true, Mama Bear, that Goldilocks was just trying to protect herself? Maybe she was just scared. After all, she's just a little girl. And your husband is a big, scary bear."

"Objection, Your Honor!" Brooke jumped to her feet. "The lawyer is harassing my witness!"

"Overruled! You may answer the question, Mama Bear," Judge Hawkings said.

"I forgot the question," Danielle said in a small voice.

"I said, Goldilocks is just a small girl. How could Goldilocks have assaulted Papa Bear? We haven't heard any testimony about Papa Bear being injured," Joelle pointed out.

Mama Bear couldn't argue with that.

Next Caitlyn, as Baby Bear, stepped up on the witness stand. She was wearing bear ears like Danielle's and pink pajamas with feet. Her hair was in pigtails and she carried a blanket and a teddy bear. She answered all of Brooke's questions about that "mean old Goldilocks" in baby talk.

"Okay, Baby Bear," Joelle said when it was her turn to speak. "I understand Goldilocks ate all your porridge."

"That's right," Caitlyn said, sucking her thumb.

"Couldn't your mom just make you some more porridge?"

"No. That was all the porridge we had."

"Couldn't she have made you something else then?"

"No. I only eat porridge."

Everyone giggled.

Joelle rolled her eyes again. "You sure are picky, Baby Bear. I bet you had some porridge the day before Goldilocks came to your house, didn't you?"

"I don't remember," Caitlyn answered, pouting.

"Come on. Mama Bear wouldn't let you go a whole day without food. When you're out of porridge, she probably goes to the store and buys more. But poor Goldilocks hadn't had anything to eat for three whole days. Didn't you feel sorry for her?"

"No. She broke my chair."

"Yes, I know," Joelle said. "It was an accident. She's terribly sorry and she's willing to buy you a new one. She doesn't really need to go to jail, does she?"

"Yes, she does!" Caitlyn insisted.

"Why?" Joelle pressed.

"Because she's *bad!*" Caitlyn hugged her teddy bear.

Joelle tried a new tactic. "You don't like humans much, do you, Baby Bear?"

"No."

"You might even be prejudiced against them."

Caitlyn bit her lip. She knew she'd made a mistake.

Ha! Joelle thought. *Got her!*

A few minutes later, it was time for Joelle to call her witnesses. All of them talked about how wonderful Goldilocks was and how shocked they were to hear she'd been accused of these crimes.

Ryan played the Bears' neighbor, Mr. Farnsworth. "The Bears are a fine family," he said in a deep, serious voice. "They keep to themselves and don't cause trouble."

"Would you say that the Bears are afraid of humans?" Joelle asked.

"Definitely," Ryan said.

"And how was Goldilocks when you found her in the woods?" Joelle asked.

"Really, really sick," Ryan said. "It was terrible."

"Thank you, Mr. Farnsworth," Joelle said.

Ian Walsh, who played the doctor, claimed that Goldilocks was hungry and dehydrated and probably not in her right mind at the time.

There wasn't much Brooke could do with these witnesses in her cross-examination.

I'm going to win this, Joelle thought triumphantly. *That'll show Brooke.*

Once all the witnesses had spoken, Brooke and Joelle gave their closing statements. Then the jury went out into the hall to make their decision.

"You all did a terrific job," Mr. Hawkings said. "It'll be interesting to see what the jury decides."

All around the room, kids were whispering.

Yes, Joelle thought. *It will be* very *interesting to see what the jury decides.* There was no doubt she'd presented the better case. She knew it and she was sure everybody else in the room knew it, too. She had just beaten the great Brooke Hartle!

Joelle glanced across the aisle and found Brooke looking back at her. Brooke actually looked worried.

Good, Joelle thought with satisfaction. *She needs to lose every once in a while.*

The jury marched back into the room, single file. They looked very serious.

"Has the jury reached a verdict?" Judge Hawkings asked.

Joelle sat up a little straighter.

The jury members all looked at each other. Then a boy stood up and said, "We have, Your Honor. We find the defendant, Goldilocks, guilty as charged."

What? Joelle's mouth dropped open.

Even Brooke looked surprised. Then a slow smile broke out across her face.

No! This can't be! Joelle told herself.

But it was.

She'd lost.

"All right!" Several kids gathered around Brooke to congratulate her.

Joelle turned away. How could the jury have found Goldilocks guilty? Didn't they listen to the testimony? Or didn't the facts matter?

Was this whole trial just some sort of popularity contest?

It wasn't fair!

The bell rang and kids charged toward the door.

Joelle stayed in her seat.

"Hey," Ryan gave her a light punch on the arm as he passed. "You did a good job."

Joelle stared at her desktop. "Right. Thanks."

"Joelle?" Ryan frowned. "What's the matter?"

Joelle turned away as tears pricked her eyes. She *never* cried. Ever.

"Why don't you go on to class, Ryan?" Mr. Hawkings said, coming over. "See you tomorrow, okay?"

Ryan nodded and left. The teacher leaned against the desk across from Joelle.

Joelle raised her eyes. "I should have won," she said tightly.

"I presented the better case."

Mr. Hawkings rubbed his mustache. "I guess the jury didn't see it that way."

"That's because they all wanted Brooke to win," Joelle said. "In a real trial, jurors make a decision based on evidence, not on personal feelings."

The teacher raised his eyebrows. "Not always. That's one of the reasons we have an appeals process."

"Okay, then. I want an appeal."

Mr. Hawkings laughed. "Don't take all this so seriously, Joelle." He patted her on the shoulder. "You did a great job. You presented a good argument. You argued your case well. And your grade will reflect that."

"I don't care about my grade!" Joelle clenched her fist under her desk in frustration. "I care about fairness."

"Nobody wins all the time, Joelle," Mr. Hawkings said. "Sometimes, in the courtroom and in life, all you can do is present your argument and see what happens. Sometimes you win and sometimes you lose. And sometimes it doesn't seem fair."

Tell me about it, Joelle thought. But she knew she couldn't just sit around like this, moping and whining.

"Thanks, Mr. Hawkings," Joelle said, getting up.

It was time to move on.

Chapter Sixteen

Joelle heard some girls talking in the bathroom later that afternoon.

About *her*. This was getting to be a habit. Did anybody in this town ever talk about anything else?

"She's such a sore loser."

"Well, I'm glad she lost. She thinks she's better than everyone else, just because she's from *Minn-e-a-pol-is!*"

Joelle peered through the crack by the stall door. Who was out there?

Shelby and Caitlyn. They were both softball players. Brooke was there, too, brushing her hair. She hadn't said anything yet.

"She's too good to play softball for Hoover. Too good to associate with us. So what does she do? She starts her own dumb league and goes over to Greendale Academy, our biggest competition, and asks *them* to play."

"You should have heard her in band," Brooke spoke up, putting her brush back in her backpack. "'Let me put this in terms you'll understand.' Like I'm stupid or something."

Joelle flushed the toilet and stormed out of the stall. "I never said you were stupid!"

All three girls jumped.

"Were you listening?" Shelby demanded.

Joelle ignored her and turned on Brooke. "So you'd rather talk about me behind my back than face to face, huh? Well, fine. Come on, what else about me bugs you? What else were you going to say?"

"Nothing." Brooke shouldered her backpack. "Let's go," she said to her friends.

Joelle stuck her arm across the door to stop them from leaving. It was time she and Brooke had it out. "Hey, I never said you were stupid," she repeated. "I just said I didn't want to play softball."

"Yeah, you've said it over and over and over. We're all getting really sick of it, too." Brooke's eyes flashed and her face was flushed under her careful makeup. "You're a *baseball* player. You're way too good to play softball."

"I never said I was too good to play softball!"

"Give me a break, Cunningham. Everything you do says it. You don't even try to fit in here. You walk around the school all high and mighty."

Joelle's jaw dropped. *"You* should talk, Brooke! You're the one who looks down on everyone else. Girls like you always have to look down on everyone else."

"What do you mean, girls like me?" Brooke's eyes narrowed. "You think you know all about me, don't you?"

"Every school has girls like you," Joelle said. "You're all the same. Popular, perfect, snobby, and mean."

To Joelle's surprise, Brooke didn't answer. She just stood there, looking stunned.

"That's what you think?" Brooke said finally. Joelle couldn't be sure, but she thought the girl's mascara was starting to run a tiny bit. Was Brooke…crying?

Joelle gulped. Maybe she'd gone a little too far.

Brooke pushed past Joelle's arm and out of the bathroom. The door swung shut behind her.

"You don't know anything, Ms. Baseball," Shelby said in a low voice. Then she and Caitlyn hurried out into the hall after Brooke.

Joelle slumped against the cold tile wall. Those girls had been jerks to talk about her like that. But she'd been a jerk, too. And she hadn't accomplished a thing.

Sometimes trying to stand up for yourself makes things a whole lot worse, Joelle told herself. *You have to do it the right way.*

And she had a feeling she had just done everything the wrong way.

* * *

"I guess you heard about what happened with me and Brooke," Joelle said to Elizabeth as the two of them walked home together after school.

Elizabeth nodded. "Yep, I heard."

"It was pretty bad," Joelle said. "I said some things I maybe shouldn't have said. But I am so tired of girls like Brooke! I can't get away from them."

"What do you mean, girls like Brooke?"

"Oh, you know. The *popular ones.* Perfect clothes, perfect hair, perfect lives. Those kids can be so mean to anyone who's just a little bit different."

"Brooke's not like that," Elizabeth said slowly.

"Well, you didn't hear her in the bathroom," Joelle said as they crossed a street.

Elizabeth didn't answer.

"You know, back in Minneapolis, some girls never understood why I liked baseball, either," Joelle went on. "They picked on me all the time. The only friends I had were boys. None of the girls liked me." There. She'd said it. "And it was all because of girls like Brooke!"

Elizabeth shifted her backpack to her other shoulder. "I've known Brooke a long time, Joelle," she said. "She's really not like you think. I mean, she's had some bad stuff happen in her life."

"Oh, what?" Joelle pretended to pout. "Has she broken a fingernail?"

Elizabeth stopped walking. "Her dad died, Joelle. He was working on their roof and he fell off and...he was paralyzed for a while and then he died."

"Oh." Joelle blinked. "I didn't know." Not that that made her like Brooke any better, but she did feel bad for her.

"It happened about three years ago," Elizabeth went on. "Brooke tries to cover things up, but it's been pretty tough for her and her mom."

"I'm really sorry," Joelle said, shaking her head. It was hard enough simply having Jason away at college. If he or anyone else in her family was...gone forever... Joelle didn't even want to think about it.

"Brooke wants to do really well in high school so she can get a college scholarship," Elizabeth said as they started walking again. "That's why she works so hard at everything all the time."

Joelle certainly understood *that*. She was probably going to need a scholarship, too. Maybe not as much as Brooke, though.

"You want to know something else?" Elizabeth asked. "I think Brooke wants to play in our league."

"You've got to be kidding." Joelle couldn't imagine Brooke on the Green Sox.

"No, really. She keeps asking me about it."

"Brooke hates me, remember?" Joelle kicked at a pebble on the sidewalk. "She would never play on the same team as me."

Elizabeth threw up her hands. "Look. Brooke doesn't get why you won't play softball. That doesn't mean she hates you, Joelle. Actually, the two of you might even be friends if you got to know each other. You're a lot alike."

"Me? Like Brooke?" *No way*, Joelle told herself.

Elizabeth nodded. "You're both really good athletes. Both smart and super competitive. And both kind of...stubborn."

"I am *not* stubborn!" Joelle said quickly. But she was. She knew she was.

"Brooke may not want to admit it, but I think she really admires you for trying so hard to play baseball here." Elizabeth's voice suddenly dropped. "And we only need one more player for the Green Sox."

"*We?*" Joelle grabbed Elizabeth's arm. "Does that mean you're going to play?"

Elizabeth blushed. "Don't change the subject, Joelle! I think

163

you should ask Brooke to join. If *you* asked her, I bet she'd say yes."

"Oh no," Joelle answered quickly. "I'm not going to go to Brooke and beg. There are signs up all over school. If she wants to play, she can come and talk to me about it."

"She's not going to do that," Elizabeth said.

"Then I guess she won't be playing with us," Joelle said, shrugging.

Elizabeth sighed. "Like I said, you're exactly alike," she muttered. "Totally stubborn."

* * *

On Saturday morning, Elizabeth's dad showed up at Center Park wearing a green sweatshirt that said COACH across the front in huge yellow letters.

"He just had that made at the sports shop," Elizabeth whispered to Joelle as they stood around waiting for practice to begin. "Isn't it awful?"

"I think it's kind of cute," Joelle said, grinning. She was glad Mr. Shaw was taking his job as coach seriously.

"Okay, Green Sox." Coach Shaw blew his whistle.

Joelle and Elizabeth both jumped. Elizabeth winced and rubbed her ear. "The whistle's new, too."

"Hello, girls," Mr. Shaw said. "It's good to see you again. As you know, I'm Elizabeth's dad, and I'm really happy to be coaching the Green Sox. I guess we all know each other by now, so why don't we get started right away?"

Everyone nodded eagerly.

Coach Shaw checked something in one of the library books he'd brought. Then he led the team through thirty minutes of bending, stretching, and running laps. It wasn't as formal as what Joelle was used to, but it was fine, especially for a first practice.

Coach Shaw wanted to get an idea of everyone's strengths and weaknesses. After warm-ups, he rotated each girl around to different positions.

Joelle paid close attention to how her teammates did at first base. She always considered first base *her* position, but she'd play whatever Coach Shaw told her to play.

Paige was pretty good at first base, too, but she wasn't as tall as Joelle. Besides, Paige and Paula seemed to play outfield best. Especially when they were out there together. They always seemed to know who was going to go for the ball and who was going to make the relay play.

Joelle thought Mandi and Leah made another good team, as pitcher and catcher. On the other hand, Leah was short and quick. She might be better suited to second base than catcher.

And Tara, with her incredible arm, definitely belonged at left field, in Joelle's opinion. Or maybe third base. She wasn't sure where Nikki and Elizabeth played best.

Coach Shaw blew his whistle again. "Okay, that's enough for today." He waved them all in from the field.

Joelle felt a little disappointed. It seemed like they'd just gotten started and now practice was over? Already? She wiped the sweat from her forehead, then jogged over to the dugout to join her friends.

"That wasn't bad for our first practice," Coach Shaw said as the girls grabbed their water bottles and equipment. "But don't go anywhere yet, Green Sox. We've got a few things to talk about. Take a look at this."

He passed around what looked like a computer-designed invitation to a little kid's birthday party. There was a ball and bat on the outside of the card. But on the inside it read: "The Chesterfield Kernels challenge the Greendale Green Sox to a game of baseball on May 3. Field to be determined. R.S.V.P."

"They're *challenging* us?" Mandi asked, cracking her gum.

"Hey, we can't turn down a challenge," Joelle said.

"But we don't have a full team," Elizabeth pointed out.

"Do they?" Nikki asked.

"They've got nine or ten players, I think," Mr. Shaw said.

"Well, I'm with Joelle," Mandi said. "We can't turn down a challenge. We'll just have to find one more player."

Elizabeth nudged Joelle. "Brooke," she whispered.

Joelle's entire body tensed.

"Who's Brooke?" Mandi asked, leaning forward.

"She's co-captain of our softball team," Elizabeth said. "And she's really good." She looked pointedly at Joelle.

"So why don't you call her, Joelle?" Leah asked.

"Yeah," several others put in.

Joelle glared at Elizabeth. She didn't want Brooke on their team! But she wasn't exactly in a position to be choosy. And Elizabeth knew that.

"Well, if we're going to ask her to join, why do *I* have to be the one to do it?" Joelle grumbled.

"Because you know her," Mandi said.

"Yeah, you go to the same school, right?" Leah put in.

"And since this whole league thing was your idea, it'll sound better coming from you." Elizabeth patted her on the back and smiled.

Joelle sighed. Strikes one, two, and three.

She was out.

* * *

Joelle sat cross-legged on the couch, the phone in her lap. She had been staring at the scrap of paper with Brooke's phone number so long that she had the number memorized. Joelle did not want to have Brooke's phone number memorized.

She sighed. Might as well get it over with.

"Hello?" Brooke answered.

"Hello, Brooke? This is, um, Joelle." Joelle's heart thumped. "Joelle Cunningham."

"I only know one Joelle," Brooke said coldly. "What do you want?"

Joelle stretched out her legs. "Listen," she began, "about the other day in the bathroom."

"Yeah."

"You said I didn't know anything about you." Joelle picked at a loose thread in the couch. "Well, you're right, I guess. I don't. You do sort of remind me of some girls I knew back home. But you're not them, so I shouldn't treat you like you are."

Silence. Maybe Brooke didn't realize that was about as close to an apology as she was going to get.

"But you know, you don't know much about me, either," Joelle went on quickly. "I don't think I'm better than anyone. I just get a little, well...obsessed with things sometimes. Like baseball." Brooke still didn't say anything.

"Anyway, this sounds kind of crazy, but Elizabeth thinks we'd probably like each other if we got to know each other."

Brooke snorted. "Ha. Right."

"That's what I said, too," Joelle said with a short laugh. She cleared her throat. "Elizabeth...um...also thinks you might want to play in our baseball league."

That got Brooke's attention. "Are you asking me to play?"

"Do you want to play?" Joelle shot back.

Pause. "I might consider it," Brooke said finally.

Joelle glared at the phone. What did she want? An engraved invitation?

"Look, we're meeting at Center Park Saturday morning at ten," Joelle said. "Come by if you want to, okay?"

"I'll think about it," Brooke answered.

Argh! Joelle banged down the receiver. Dealing with that girl was so frustrating. Why couldn't she just say "Sure, that sounds great!" instead of leaving everyone to wonder whether she'd be there or not?

The weird thing was, Joelle sort of hoped Brooke would decide to come.

* * *

Brooke did show up for practice on Saturday. Her hair was pulled back in a ponytail and she wore purple sweats with a plain white T-shirt.

Joelle nodded to Brooke and Brooke nodded back. What else

was there to say? Brooke would probably change her mind about playing baseball anyway. She might not even join the team.

After the other girls and Elizabeth's dad introduced themselves to Brooke, they started on warm-ups.

"I hope you guys do a lot of fielding drills," Brooke said to Joelle as she stretched out in a straddle position. "Everybody likes to bat, but fielding is important, too. If you can't field, you'll never get up to bat in the first place."

Brooke wasn't going to try and run everything, was she? Joelle gritted her teeth and kept stretching.

"Uh oh. Look over there." Mandi pointed at some kids heading their way. They were carrying bats and balls.

Anyone could use the fields in Center Park. It was first-come, first-serve.

"Quick!" Joelle leaped to her feet. "Let's get set up. That way they'll see this field's in use."

"We can't skip warm-ups!" Brooke protested.

"We're not skipping them. We're just moving them over to the field," Joelle said.

Luckily, the newcomers got the message. They turned and headed for the playground equipment instead.

"Don't you guys run laps?" Brooke asked.

"Of course we run laps." Joelle rolled her eyes. "Some of us even run every day outside of practice."

Brooke stretched her left quad muscle. "Good," she said. "You know, we should probably—"

This was getting too annoying. "Listen, Brooke, you may be captain of the softball team, but you're not captain here!" Joelle said. The other girls all stared at her.

Brooke paused. "Oh. Right. So are *you* the captain, then?" she asked.

"Well, no," Joelle admitted.

"No one is," Leah spoke up.

"Fine," Brooke said, shrugging. "Then I guess anyone can make suggestions."

Elizabeth touched Joelle's arm. "Lighten up," she whispered. "We're a team, remember?"

Joelle sighed. "Yeah. I know." And if Brooke was going to be part of that team, the two of them were going to have to find a way to get along.

Coach Shaw led them through some routine drills. Joelle had to admit, Brooke wasn't bad. Like Elizabeth said, the girl could hit just about anything. Whatever Mandi threw, she hit.

Brooke was an aggressive fielder, too. She wasn't afraid of the ball. Line drives or pop flies, her glove was always right there. And she didn't hesitate to run when she had to, either.

There was one pop fly that Joelle was sure Brooke would miss. She ran hard, then leaped up, her arm outstretched. The ball dropped into her glove as she fell to the ground.

"Nice catch," Joelle called.

Brooke scrambled to her feet and threw the ball to Nikki. "Gee, thanks," she said coolly as she brushed the grass from her sweats.

"Hey, I'm trying here," Joelle said. "If we're going to be on the same team, you'll have to try, too."

Brooke shrugged and turned away. "Whatever," she said.

Chapter Seventeen

S o, let's talk uniforms," Brooke said when practice was over.

Joelle squirted some water into her mouth, then wiped the back of her arm across her face. Brooke had been a member of the Green Sox for less than two hours and already she was worried about what they would *wear?*

"Good point," Mandi said, nodding. "If we're going to play the Kernels next week, we need uniforms."

Well, that was true, Joelle had to admit.

"What do you have in mind?" Coach Shaw asked Brooke.

Brooke thought for a minute. "I don't know. As long as it's not orange, I don't really care. Everyone looks awful in orange."

Joelle rolled her eyes. "We're the *Green* Sox," she said. "Shouldn't we just wear green?"

"How about gray sweatpants and green T-shirts?" Leah suggested.

"Yeah," Nikki agreed. "We could probably all get those before next week."

"Okay, that's settled," Brooke said. "What about publicity?

We'll really need to get the word out about this game. Tell everyone we know. Put up posters. Send out press releases to the *Gazette*, the radio stations, and Channel 6. Maybe we could even have a big party after the game. And—"

"Whoa there, hold on a minute!" Coach Shaw chuckled and held up his hands to stop Brooke. "This is just an informal game. I don't think we need to make too big a fuss about it. We certainly don't need to issue press releases."

"Why not?" Brooke pulled the purple scrunchi off her pony-tail and ran her fingers through her hair. "If we make a huge deal about this game, it'll show people we're really serious."

We? Joelle raised her eyebrows. Brooke was sure throwing herself into things now.

"Plus, if other girls see us in the paper or on TV, it'll make them want to play, too," Brooke went on. "Isn't that sort of the goal? To get more people to join?" She turned to Joelle. "What do you think?"

Everyone looked at Joelle.

Joelle cleared her throat. Nothing like being put on the spot. "I…uh…agree with Brooke," she said. "I guess." From the corner of her eye, Joelle saw Elizabeth smile.

* * *

At school on Monday, kids were already starting to talk about the Green Sox's first game. One thing Joelle had to say for Brooke, she got things going.

Fast.

By Wednesday, there were Green Sox posters up in the

school lobby, the library, the gym, and all over the cafeteria. On Thursday night, Brooke and Elizabeth even got a few of their softball teammates to help them make a green and yellow felt Green Sox banner. The next morning it was hanging next to the trophy case beside the main office.

Ryan caught up with Joelle between classes on Friday. "So, you guys did it," he said. "You're playing your first game. Congrats."

Joelle felt herself blush. "Well, we could still use a few more players," she said. "And we're just playing at Center Park. But it's a start. Are you going to come watch our game?" The words slipped out before Joelle could stop them. She hoped she didn't sound too eager.

But she'd gone to the guys' games, right?

To her relief, Ryan nodded. "Yeah, a bunch of us will probably go," he replied. "We'll cheer you on."

"Great! Thanks." Joelle couldn't keep the excitement out of her voice. The more people who showed up to offer support, the better. And knowing that Ryan would be there made her sort of happy, too.

* * *

On Saturday morning, Joelle could hardly believe her eyes when she and her parents pulled up in front of Center Park. Cars lined both sides of the street. Groups of people crowded the sidewalks. Some carried folding chairs. Others waved homemade signs that said Go Green Sox! or Go Kernels! It was a total mob scene.

"We'd better let you out here," Joelle's dad said. "I don't know how far away we'll have to park."

"Okay," Joelle said. She adjusted the visor of her new green cap. "I bet there are more people here than were at our playoff game in Minneapolis last year."

Mom smiled. "Maybe," she said.

"Well, that's good," Dad said. "It shows folks are really interested in girls' baseball."

"I sure hope so." Joelle grabbed her glove and got out of the car. "See you later," she called to her parents over her shoulder.

"Can you believe this crowd?" Mandi asked as she and Leah ran toward Joelle. "It's making me kind of nervous."

"It's incredible," Joelle said, looking around. She spotted a huge group of Hoover kids in the middle of the crowd. Ms. Fenner and her mother sat in folding chairs right behind the field. And back by the trees, she saw Ryan Carlyle and several guys from the Hawks team.

"Wow. There are even TV people here!" Mandi pointed at two cameramen setting up over by the playing field. They were wearing Channel 6 jackets.

"We're going to be stars!" Leah said, pulling off her cap and pretending to adjust her hair.

Joelle was thrilled the TV people had shown up. But at the same time, she wondered how Brooke was able to get them to come. Joelle hadn't even been able to get one lousy newspaper person to show up at their organizational meeting.

Two girls came up to Joelle, Mandi, and Leah. One wore her hair in a long red braid. The other had short brown hair. Both were dressed in matching yellow T-shirts and black sweat-pants and each carried a bat and a glove.

Kernels, Joelle told herself.

"Excuse me, is one of you Joelle Cunningham?" the red-haired girl asked.

"I am," Joelle answered. "And these are my friends Mandi and Leah."

"Hi, I'm Lauren," said the girl with the braid. She pointed to the other girl. "This is Sami. We're the enemy," she added with a grin.

"We just wanted to tell you how glad we are that you started this whole league," Sami said. She smiled and a dimple appeared in her left cheek.

"We also figured we should warn you that you're about to get creamed," Lauren put in.

Joelle and Mandi glanced at each other.

"Really?" Mandi said with a straight face. "But aren't we playing you guys?" She scrunched her eyebrows together, pre-tending to be confused.

"Very funny," Lauren said. She stuck out her hand. "May the best team win."

Joelle shook Lauren's hand. "We intend to," she said.

"Excuse me." A man in khaki pants and a Greendale Parks and Rec T-shirt made his way through the crowd. "Who is in charge here?"

The girls all looked at each other.

"Um, that's our coach, Mr. Shaw, over there." Joelle pointed at Elizabeth's dad, who was talking with some men over by home plate. Elizabeth was with them. "He's in charge of the Green Sox, anyway."

"And Coach Kennedy is in charge of the Kernels. She's over there." Lauren pointed across the field.

"Thanks." The man nodded and headed over to Coach Shaw.

"Who's he?" Sami asked.

"I don't know." Joelle bit her lip. For some reason, she had a bad feeling about this.

The girls watched as the man said something to Elizabeth's dad. Coach Shaw's smile disappeared. He called to Coach Kennedy and motioned for her to join them.

The Parks and Rec guy talked to both coaches for a few minutes. Joelle could see Coach Kennedy's frown from way back where she stood. Then both coaches started arguing with the man, but he just sort of shrugged and held up his hands. Elizabeth stood behind her dad, biting her lip.

"What's going on over there?" Lauren asked.

Joelle shook her head. "I don't know," she said, but her heart was pounding. Elizabeth's dad looked really annoyed now. Whatever it was, it obviously wasn't good.

Finally the Parks and Rec guy cupped his hands around his mouth and called to the crowd, "Listen up, everyone! I know you're all here to see the baseball game, but it will not be played here today!"

"What?" Joelle, Mandi, Lauren and Sami all cried at the same time.

There was a collective gasp from the crowd. Everyone looked confused.

"I repeat, this game is not going to be played here today. Please exit the park in an orderly fashion."

That was when Joelle noticed the police officers standing behind the fence.

What was the problem? Had they done something wrong? It had to be some kind of mistake.

The TV people quickly hoisted cameras on their shoulders. One of the reporters stuck a microphone in the Parks and Rec guy's face as he walked off the field. "No comment," he said. He pushed the microphone away and headed quickly out of the park.

The police officers stepped forward and began to direct people out of the area.

Then people started yelling. "What's going on? What happened? Why is the game being canceled? When will it be rescheduled?"

But no one had any answers.

Joelle and Mandi made their way over to Coach Shaw and the other Green Sox and their parents.

"What happened?" Joelle demanded. "Why can't we play?"

Elizabeth's dad sighed. "It seems that the Greendale Parks and Recreation Department feels that Center Park isn't a suitable place to hold a baseball game for a group this size."

"Oh, come on!" an older boy scoffed. "That's stupid."

"Why not?" a woman asked.

"There's a baseball diamond here, isn't there?" one of the Kernels said. "And this is a public park. How can they say we can't use it?"

177

"The Rec department pointed out that this is a small park in a residential area," Coach Shaw explained, scratching the back of his neck. "Apparently the baseball diamond is for neighborhood use only. It's not intended for large groups. It can't be reserved.

"So the Parks and Rec people are concerned about safety issues and liability," Joelle's dad said.

"There are too many people here today, I'm afraid," Coach Shaw added. "There isn't any fencing around the diamond itself. And ultimately, the city owns the park, so they get to make the rules."

"But that's not fair!" Joelle cried. *They were so close to having a real league!*

"I'm sorry," Coach Shaw said. "It never occurred to me that we'd have to get permission. I just assumed that Central Park was for community use."

"And there's no other place we can play," Mandi said glumly. "We can't play at any of the schools because we're not a school activity."

"Maybe we could become a Parks and Rec activity," Joelle suggested hopefully.

"I already spoke to them about that last week," Mandi's dad said. "Unfortunately, they don't have enough fields for the baseball and softball programs they already offer."

"Okay, so where *can* we play?" Tara wanted to know.

"A few kids play ball at this big empty lot in my neighborhood," Brooke said. "Maybe we could play there."

Coach Shaw looked doubtful. "Empty or not, somebody

still owns that property. We can't just start playing there without permission from the owners."

"So let's find out who owns the property and see if we can get their permission," Brooke said.

Joelle glanced at Brooke from under the visor of her cap. She had to give her credit for trying to find solutions.

"Well, I suppose it would be easy enough to find out who owns the property," Coach Shaw said. "But I have a feeling they'll have the same concerns as the Parks and Rec department. They won't want the liability."

Joelle kicked at a pebble on the ground. This league just wasn't going to happen. She might as well face facts.

It was over.

"You know, there's nothing to stop you girls from getting together and playing informally," Coach Shaw said, trying to sound cheerful.

"You mean just give up on the league?" Brooke cried.

Joelle looked up in surprise. It sounded like Brooke cared about this league almost as much Joelle did.

Coach Shaw shrugged. "I'm afraid we don't have much choice."

"We should at least find out who owns that lot and go talk to them," Brooke said firmly.

"How would we do that?" Mandy asked.

"Well," Coach Shaw said doubtfully, "the courthouse has property records, but—"

"Fine," Brooke interrupted. "We'll go to the courthouse. Who's coming with me?"

None of the Green Sox answered right away. Joelle looked around.

Elizabeth was biting her lip again. Tara was scowling. Everyone looked completely discouraged.

But if Brooke wasn't tossing in the towel, neither was Joelle. "I'll come with you," she spoke up.

Brooke looked at Joelle and nodded. If she was disappointed that Joelle was the only one who volunteered to go with her, she didn't show it. "Okay," Brooke said. "We'll go to the courthouse on Monday."

"Don't you have softball on Monday?" Joelle asked. "The courthouse will be closed by the time practice is over."

"I can miss practice just this once," Brooke said.

Whoa! Joelle decided not to comment on that. "Well, okay then. We'll go on Monday."

* * *

Later that afternoon, Joelle lay across her bed on her back, tossing Jason's tournament ball up in the air and catching it. Up, down. Up, down. Monday seemed like a long way away. What if Coach Shaw was right? What if they found the owner of the lot, but the person refused to give them permission to play ball on their property? What then? Where else could they go?

The phone rang. "Honey?" Joelle's mom called up the stairs. "It's for you!"

Joelle rolled off the bed and took the call across the hall in the den. "Hello?"

"Joelle? It's Mandi. Are you watching Channel 6?"

"No. Why?"

"Turn it on," Mandi demanded. "Now!"

Joelle looked around for the remote. She couldn't find it, so she hurried across the room and turned on the TV by hand.

"Do you have it yet?" Mandi asked impatiently.

Joelle pressed the channel-down button on the TV until she got to Channel 6.

"Okay. I've got it. Oh, my gosh!" Joelle drew in her breath. Coach Shaw was on TV! And Coach Kennedy. And the man from Greendale Parks and Rec.

"I repeat, this game is not going to be played here today. Please exit the park in an orderly fashion," the Parks and Rec guy was saying.

Joelle cringed. It was bad enough having lived through that once. She didn't need to see it again. But she couldn't *not* watch, either.

Next they showed the police officers ushering people out of the park while several of the Kernels stood around with dazed expressions on their faces. Then they cut back to Tamara Macon and Mike Morgan in the studio.

"Those were some pretty disappointed girls, folks," Tamara said, turning in her chair to face the camera.

"I'm sure they were," Mike said. "So what's going to happen now? Are these girls going to be able to play baseball somewhere else?"

"Well, Mike, nobody seems to know for sure," Tamara answered. "But we'll be following this story very closely in the days and weeks to come."

"Thanks, Tamara. And in other news—"

Joelle switched off the TV.

"So? What do you think?" Mandi asked.

"I don't know," Joelle said slowly. "I can't believe we made the five o'clock news!"

"Well, it's just the local station," Mandi said. "They're pretty desperate for news."

Still, Joelle thought. The fact that the Eastern Iowa Girls' Baseball League had made any news at all meant people were hearing about them. You couldn't buy that kind of publicity.

But would it do any good? Joelle wondered. Or was it too little too late?

Chapter Eighteen

The phone rang again during dinner. Joelle jumped up and grabbed it before her mother could object. Maybe it was one of the Green Sox, calling with good news. "Hello?" she said through a mouthful of mashed potatoes.

"Joelle, this is Coach Carlyle."

Joelle stopped chewing. Why would *Ryan's* dad be calling *her?*

Coach Carlyle cleared his throat. "I just got off the phone with Superintendent Holland. Apparently the school board has been having discussions about your wanting to play baseball. It sounds like the rules are about to be changed."

Joelle nearly dropped the phone. She swallowed the rest of the potato in her mouth. "You mean they're going to let girls play baseball?" Just like that?

"I guess so," Coach Carlyle said. "If you still want to play, show up Monday after school and we'll see what you've got." Then he hung up.

Joelle just stood there in stunned silence.

I did it! she thought. *I got the school district to change their stupid policy!*

Except…she couldn't go to any practice on Monday. What was she thinking? She and Brooke were going downtown to find out who owned that empty lot. Brooke was even skipping softball to go. So how could Joelle go to a Hawks practice?

"What was that about, honey?" Mom asked when Joelle returned to the table.

"That was Coach Carlyle. From the Hawks. They're going to let me play."

"What?" Dad cried, jumping up from his chair. "That's great!" He threw his arms around Joelle.

Mom grabbed Joelle's hand and squeezed it hard. "That's terrific, honey. That's what you wanted."

"Yeah," Joelle said.

It was *exactly* what she'd wanted when she first moved here. So why wasn't she more excited?

* * *

"Why don't you and Brooke go downtown another day?" Mom suggested later that evening. She and Joelle were folding clothes in the laundry room.

Joelle leaned against the drier. "No. We have to go Monday." She and Brooke had already made plans. She couldn't very well call Brooke up and say sorry, I can't make it. Not now. Besides, if they didn't go Monday, when would they go? The softball team practiced every day but Wednesday. The Hawks practiced every day but Thursday.

"Well, if the coach told you to show up on Monday, I think you need to be there," Mom said. She tossed a folded blouse onto the pile on the drier.

Joelle picked up the green T-shirt she'd worn on Saturday. Mom was probably right. The funny thing was, after everything she'd been through, Joelle wasn't sure playing baseball for the Hawks was still so important to her.

For one thing, she wasn't convinced Coach Carlyle really wanted her to play. The school board had changed their policy. That meant Coach Carlyle had to give her a chance. It didn't mean he wanted to. Did she really want to play for a coach who didn't want her?

Part of her did. Part of her wanted to prove to the Hawks coach and everyone else that she belonged. And that girls could play baseball.

But part of her wanted to just walk away. She had the Green Sox now. Even though they didn't have a field, didn't have teams to play against, and didn't have a whole lot of support, they were still a team. They were *her* team. It almost felt disloyal to play for anyone else.

But what would people say if Joelle didn't play for the Hawks now that she had the chance? They'd probably figure she hadn't been that serious about it in the first place. Or maybe they'd think she was some space case who changed her mind at the drop of a hat.

"Joelle?" Mom said. "What are you thinking?"

"I don't know," Joelle answered in a small voice. It was hard to put her thoughts into words.

Mom peered closer at Joelle. "What is it, honey?"

Joelle sank down onto the cold, hard, cement floor. "This may sound weird, but I'm not sure I want to play for the Hawks anymore," she said finally.

"What?" Mom came over to Joelle. "Why not?"

Joelle shrugged and picked at a scab on her ankle. "I loved playing for the Blue Jays back in Minneapolis, but it's not going to be the same with the Hawks."

Mom sat down next to Joelle. "Well, that's true, honey. No two teams are exactly the same. That's because the people involved with the teams are different. But you'll find your place with the Hawks."

"Maybe." Joelle clasped her knees. "I never really thought about the fact that all the other players on the Blue Jays were guys. I don't think they thought about me being a girl, either. I was just Joelle. But here I think I'd always be the girl they had to let on the team."

"Not necessarily," Mom said. "Not once your teammates get to know you."

"Back in Minneapolis, everybody already knew me because I was Jason Cunningham's little sister. That made things so much easier."

Whoa. Wait a minute! Joelle thought suddenly. She turned to face her mother. "Do you think they let me play in Minneapolis because I was Jason's sister?" Had she been riding on Jason's reputation her entire life?

"No, of course not!" Mom shook her head. "It's true that everybody knew your brother. But you earned your spot on the team just like all the other players."

"I guess," Joelle said. But what if she'd had a big brother

who was into art or music or something else? Would she still have played baseball herself or would she have played softball? Maybe she wouldn't have played either one. Her whole life might have been totally different.

"You've had to find your own way here in Greendale, Joelle," Mom said. "And I know that hasn't always been easy. But it's been good for you, don't you think?"

"Maybe," Joelle admitted. It was true. Everything she'd done in her new town so far, she'd done on her own. Even trying to change people's minds about girls playing baseball. And that had nothing to do with Jason.

"I really like playing with the Green Sox, Mom," Joelle said. It's great being on an all-girls team."

"But remember, Joelle, the Green Sox may never even get off the ground," her mother pointed out.

"I know." Joelle nodded.

"Well, it's your decision, honey," Mom said, putting an arm around her. "But you're going to have to figure something out by Monday. And you need to talk to that coach. You can't just not show up on Monday."

Joelle's mind was spinning. Did she still want to play baseball for the Hawks or didn't she?

* * *

"Congrats, Joelle!" Ryan caught up with her between first and second period at school on Monday. "I heard they're going to let you play on the Hawks now. That's great!"

"Yeah." Joelle hugged her books tighter to her chest. She

knew what she had to do today, but she still hadn't made any decisions about tomorrow. Assuming Coach Carlyle would even let her start a day late.

"See you after school then!" Ryan grinned as he turned and started toward his next class.

"No, wait!" Joelle called him back. "I, um, can't make it to practice today."

Ryan stopped and frowned. "What do you mean?" he asked as kids hurried by them.

"I have something I need to do after school. Something for the Green Sox." Joelle had a hard time looking Ryan in the eye.

Ryan walked back toward her. "You can't skip practice, Joelle. Especially not on your first day. My dad will freak."

"Well, I'll talk to him about it," Joelle said, lifting her chin.

Ryan shook his head. "If you don't show up, there won't be anything to talk about. He won't let you be on the team if you skip practice. Trust me on that."

"I wouldn't be skipping practice. I'd just be starting a day late," Joelle said. *If I decide to play at all,* she added to herself.

Ryan just stared at her. "I don't get it," he said. "I thought you wanted to play baseball."

"I do!"

"Well, you sure don't act like it. Everyone changed the rules for you, Joelle! And then you act like that's no big deal. You think you can just show up for practice when you feel like it?"

Joelle could see how it might look like she was being difficult, but that wasn't it. Not really. "The girls' baseball league is really important to me, Ryan," she said. "I'll do whatever it takes to help get it off the ground."

"So, if something else comes up with the Green Sox, you'd blow off Hawks practice again?"

Well, yeah, Joelle realized. *I probably would.* She hated the way Ryan was looking at her right now. Like she was some ditzy girl.

He didn't understand. But she couldn't lie to him. Back in Minneapolis, there was nothing she would have blown off practice for. Absolutely nothing. And when Joelle thought about it, that sort of put things into perspective.

She didn't belong on the Hawks.

She belonged with the Green Sox.

Maybe the Green Sox would never play a real game. But that wouldn't be because Joelle Cunningham gave up.

* * *

"I heard you blew off the Hawks to do this today," Brooke said to Joelle when the two of them were walking downtown that afternoon.

Of course Brooke had heard about her skipping baseball practice, Joelle thought. *It would probably be on Channel 6 at five o'clock.*

"Well?" Brooke prompted.

"Is it possible to go to the *bathroom* in this town without everybody else hearing about it in two seconds?" she asked.

Brooke laughed. "Nope. That's why I can't wait to move far away from here when I'm older."

Joelle didn't quite know what to say to that. Was Brooke unhappy here in Greendale, too? Neither of them said anything for the next block.

They came to a stoplight and Joelle pressed the WALK

button. "You skipped softball to do this," Joelle pointed out. "So why is it such a big deal if I blew off baseball?"

"It wasn't my first day of practice," Brooke said. She reached out and gave the button another push.

"So? You're the captain. You shouldn't skip practice any day."

The light changed and the girls started across the street.

Brooke shrugged. "One practice isn't such a big deal. Not if what you're doing instead is really important."

"Why is the Green Sox so important to you?" Joelle asked.

"Why is it so important to *you?*" Brooke shot back.

That was a good question. Joelle had to think about it for a minute. Finally she said, "I don't know. Because it was my idea and then it got a whole lot bigger? Does that make sense?"

Brooke nodded. "It isn't just about playing baseball for you anymore, is it?"

"No," Joelle admitted. It was also about friendship and loyalty and building something from the ground up.

Neither girl spoke for a while after that. When they reached the courthouse, Brooke turned to Joelle. "You know what?" she said with a grin. "You're all right, Cunningham."

Surprised, Joelle answered, "You're not so bad yourself, Hartle."

Together they climbed the stairs and went inside the building. Like Coach Shaw had said, it was easy enough to find out who owned a piece of land. All you had to do was fill out a short form and that was it. Property holdings were a matter of public record.

"Millie Holmes," Brooke read from the piece of paper in her hand as she and Joelle walked back outside.

"Do you know her?" Joelle asked hopefully.

Brooke shook her head. "No. But she lives at 2300 West Park Street. That's not very far from here. Come on."

"What? We're going over to her house right now?" Joelle asked.

"Sure. Why not?"

Why not indeed! Joelle picked up her pace to match Brooke's. "What are we going to say to this woman when she comes the door?"

"We'll think of something," Brooke said with a shrug. A few blocks later, she turned and marched up to a little brick bungalow. Joelle was right there beside her.

Brooke gave the door a rap with the brass knocker. Joelle crossed her fingers for good luck.

A small, elderly woman came to the door. "Yes?" she asked. Her voice was strong and clear. "May I help you girls?"

Joelle and Brooke both started talking at once. "I'm Joelle Cunningham—"

"I'm Brooke Hartle—"

They stopped and looked at one another. Then, Brooke motioned for Joelle to go ahead.

"I-I'm Joelle Cunningham and this is Brooke Hartle," Joelle repeated, stammering a little. "We're students at Hoover Middle School and we're trying to get a girls' baseball league started in this district."

"Oh yes," Mrs. Holmes said. "The ladies in my book group

have been following your story." She opened her door and let them in. "What can I do for you?"

Once they were all seated on Mrs. Holmes's old-fashioned couch, Joelle started right in. She talked about how hard they'd worked to put together a league. Then Brooke told the older woman that there weren't enough fields in Greendale for all the baseball and softball teams. And she mentioned the empty lot in her neighborhood.

"We know it's actually your property, Mrs. Holmes," Brooke rushed on. "But kids have been playing ball there for as long as I can remember. So we were sort of hoping that you'd give us permission to hold practices and play some of our games there."

Brooke sat back on the couch. She looked like she was holding her breath, waiting for an answer. Joelle could hear the loud *tick-tocks* from the grandfather clock in the hall.

"Well, I don't know," Mrs. Holmes said thoughtfully. "Harold and I had always planned to build on that lot. But now that Harold is gone, I'm not sure what to do with the property. Let me talk to my lawyer and see what he says."

Joelle's heart sank when she heard the word "lawyer." Lawyers knew about all the terrible things that could go wrong if people played on someone's property. The lawyer would probably say no. And so would Mrs. Holmes.

But Mrs. Holmes seemed like the kind of woman who gathered information and then made her own decision. Maybe she'd say yes.

They could hope, anyway.

What else could they do?

Chapter Nineteen

Joelle knew she had to talk to Coach Carlyle. She couldn't just let him assume she'd changed her mind about playing for the Hawks. She had to tell him the truth. Face to face. And that wasn't going to be easy.

"Do you want me to go with you?" Elizabeth asked her before school on Tuesday morning.

"No." Joelle took a deep breath. "This is something I have to do on my own. Will you wait for me outside his office, though?"

"Sure." Elizabeth squeezed Joelle's hand, then walked a little way down the hall.

Joelle knocked on Coach Carlyle's door.

"It's open," he called.

Joelle swallowed hard, then went inside. The coach was entering stats into his computer. He didn't even look up.

Joelle cleared her throat.

"Yes?" Finally the coach turned around. There was no expression on his face whatsoever.

Joelle had gone over what she wanted to say again and again in her mind. But somehow she couldn't remember how her little speech was supposed to begin.

"Can I help you?" Coach Carlyle asked.

"Um…" Joelle fidgeted with the strap on her backpack. "I just wanted to say…it was nice of you to give me a chance to play for the Hawks, but…I don't think I'm going to play. Not this year, anyway…"

"Okay," Coach Carlyle replied. He turned back to his computer.

Okay? Wait a minute! Didn't he at least want to know *why* she wasn't going to play? Was he that mad at her for not showing up yesterday? Ryan had warned her that his dad didn't give second chances.

But Coach Carlyle didn't look angry. He didn't look glad, either. He just looked…like he didn't care.

"Was there something else?" Coach Carlyle asked when he realized Joelle was still standing there.

Joelle frowned. Maybe none of this was ever about *her.* Maybe Coach Carlyle was just following the rules when he told her she couldn't play. And then again when he said she could play. Maybe he personally didn't care one way or the other whether she was on the team or not. She'd never even considered that possibility.

"No. I guess not." Joelle turned around and left. What more was there to say?

She saw Elizabeth at the end of the hall surrounded by a group of kids. Ian, Caitlyn, and Stephanie. And they were all talking about her. *Again.* None of them had seen her yet.

"So, she's not going to play for the Hawks at all?" Ian asked. He actually looked disappointed.

"I think maybe she wants to concentrate on the girls' baseball league," Elizabeth explained.

Joelle stopped and leaned against the wall. Should she just walk up to them? Or stay put and listen?

"I saw the Green Sox on TV," Stephanie said. "They got kicked off the field at their first game."

"Yeah, that was so unfair!" Caitlyn put in.

"Well, we haven't given up yet," Elizabeth said. "Joelle and Brooke are still trying to find us a place to play."

"Are *you* on the Green Sox, Elizabeth?" Caitlyn asked, sounding surprised.

"Actually," Elizabeth said, "I am."

Joelle smiled to herself. *Way to go, Elizabeth,* she told her friend silently.

"But you're not really a jock," Caitlyn said.

Joelle opened her mouth to protest. It was one thing for kids to say stuff to her, but she wasn't going to let anyone put Elizabeth down.

But before Joelle got a single word out, Elizabeth spoke up on her own. "You don't have to be a jock to play in our league. You just have to like baseball."

Joelle stopped short again. She'd never heard Elizabeth sound so confident.

"Well, that's great! Good for you!" Stephanie said to Elizabeth. Caitlyn nodded.

"I hope you guys find a field," Ian said. Then he, Stephanie, and Caitlyn moved on.

Elizabeth stayed behind. "Hey," she said when she noticed Joelle. "How did it go with Coach Carlyle?"

"Okay. No big deal," Joelle answered. "I heard what you said just now. Does that mean you're going to stick with the Green Sox?"

"Yeah," Elizabeth said as they started down the hall together. "I guess it does. I know I'm never going to be the best player on the team, Joelle. But I like playing. And I like hanging out with you guys. So as long as nobody expects any miracles, I'm in."

"Excellent!" Joelle turned to her friend. "And you know what, Elizabeth? You just might surprise yourself out there on the field sometime."

Yeah, right," Elizabeth said, blushing. "Like I said, no miracles, okay?"

"Okay," Joelle said. But as far as she was concerned, miracles were always possible. Especially when you worked hard and believed in yourself.

* * *

To Joelle's disappointment, there was still no word from Mrs. Holmes a few days later. How long did it take to talk to a lawyer, anyway?

"I almost wish she'd just tell us no so we can move on and figure something else out," Joelle grumbled as she poured her cereal on Tuesday morning.

"Be patient, honey," Mom said as she kissed the top of Joelle's head. She was heading off to work. "These things take time."

Joelle reached for the milk carton. Patience had never been one of her virtues.

The good news was, last Saturday's TV coverage had created a lot of interest in their league. People were calling and asking how they could get involved. Others were sending cards and letters offering support. Some even sent money.

"Don't give up," Dad said. "Something will work out."

"Hey, do I ever give up?" Joelle asked as she spooned cereal into her mouth.

That night after supper, Joelle was carrying her dishes back to the kitchen when she saw Elizabeth charging through the backyard. Before Joelle could even set her plate on the counter, Elizabeth had hopped up onto the Cunningham's deck and started pounding frantically on their sliding glass door.

Joelle's dad came into the kitchen behind Joelle. "Where's the fire?" he asked with a chuckle as he let Elizabeth in.

Joelle had never seen Elizabeth so excited. "You're never going to believe this!" her friend gasped. "My dad just got off the phone with some lawyer guy. He has to sign some papers, but we can use that field near Brooke's house. The lady you guys went to see said *yes!*"

"She did?" Joelle rushed to give Elizabeth a hug. The two of them danced around the kitchen, nearly knocking the dishes off the counter.

"All right!" Joelle's dad said.

"That's wonderful news!" her mom exclaimed, coming to the door.

"And guess what else?" Elizabeth said. "Our game with the Kernels is rescheduled. For this coming Saturday!"

"Yes!" Joelle cried, punching one fist in the air. She and Elizabeth started spinning through the kitchen again.

"Well, girls, maybe this league of yours is finally a go," Joelle's dad said.

Maybe? Joelle thought. *No way.* There was no stopping the Eastern Iowa Girls' Baseball League now!

* * *

On Friday after the Hoover softball practice, the Green Sox got together for one last time before the big game. Elizabeth's dad led them through endless drills. Hitting. Running. Catching. Fielding.

"Take it easy," he warned Brooke and Elizabeth. "We can't have you too tired to play tomorrow."

"No problem," Brooke assured him. "We'll be going on adrenaline anyway."

Coach Shaw had been trying all the girls in different positions, but he seemed to prefer Mandi as pitcher, Nikki as catcher, and the twins as outfielders. Everyone else moved around a lot.

Brooke and Joelle took turns playing first and third.

Joelle was dying to know whether she'd get to play first base in tomorrow's game. A few times she almost asked Coach Shaw straight out, but she didn't want to be too pushy.

"Keep your weight on your back foot," Coach Shaw called to Elizabeth as she came up to bat.

"Get your glove all the way to the ground," he told Tara.

"Take a strike first," he instructed Leah.

When practice was over, Coach Shaw called everyone over for a team meeting. There was a big brown box sitting on the bench behind the dugout.

"Hey, Coach! What's in the box?" Mandi asked as all the Green Sox dropped down on the grass.

Coach Shaw smiled. He opened up the carton and pulled out a pair of white pants, which he threw to Mandi. Then he handed Brooke a green shirt with three-quarter sleeves and tossed a yellow overshirt with green trim to Joelle. Finally, he produced a pair of green socks and a green cap with yellow trim.

"What's all this?" Joelle asked as she held the shirt up to her chest. It had a green number three on the back.

"Uniforms?" Leah leaned over to get a closer look inside the box. "For all of us?"

"Yeah, but where did they come from?" Joelle wanted to know.

Coach Shaw just kept smiling—and pulling out more shirts, pants, socks, and caps.

"There's a card," he said when everything had been handed out. He pulled a white envelope from the bottom of the box and gave it to Tara. She opened the envelope and read the card inside. "'To the girls of the Green Sox: I've been trying to figure out a way that I could help ever since I first heard about you. When I saw you on TV last week, the answer came to me. I hope you like the uniforms. And I hope they fit! Good luck.'" Tara looked up. "It's signed 'Claire Fenner'."

"Ms. Fenner?" Joelle said, confused. "What's she talking about? But she's already helping. She said she'd help coach this summer."

"No, not *Ms.* Fenner." Elizabeth shook her head. "Ms. Fenner's *mom.*"

"Wow, that's really nice of her," Brooke said.

"It sure is," Joelle said. She traced the number three on her shirt with her fingers.

Coach Shaw closed up the empty box. "I talked to Coach Kennedy earlier today. Her girls received a similar package from another person who saw us on TV last week. A friend of Mrs. Fenner's, I believe."

"So not everybody thinks our league is a terrible idea," Joelle said.

"There are plenty of folks who think it's a terrific idea," Coach Shaw said. "Let's just see what happens at the game tomorrow." He checked his watch. "Right now, I have to get to the library. I'm meeting with the other league coaches and sponsors. See you at home, honey." He ruffled Elizabeth's hair.

Joelle, Elizabeth, and Brooke headed out of the park together.

"So, are you guys ready for tomorrow?" Brooke asked cheerfully as she hoisted her backpack onto her back.

"Yeah," Joelle replied. "Except I wish Coach Shaw had given us our positions."

"Me, too," Brooke replied. "I'm really hoping he'll put me on first base."

Joelle stopped walking. "You want to play first base?"

"Sure, I play first in softball."

Great, Joelle thought. But she didn't say anything.

Brooke flipped her hair over her shoulder and peered at Joelle. "Why? Do you want first base, too?"

"Sort of." *I've only played that position my whole life,* Joelle thought.

"Well, I guess it's up to Coach Shaw to decide," Brooke said. "See you guys tomorrow." She waved as she turned down Park Ridge Road.

Joelle and Elizabeth kept walking on E Avenue. "Why didn't you tell me Brooke played first, too?" Joelle muttered.

Elizabeth grinned. "One more thing you have in common, huh?"

"Very funny." Joelle elbowed Elizabeth and tried not to smile back. At least she and Brooke had come to some sort of truce now. And Joelle really didn't want to keep butting heads with that girl. She just...wanted to play first base.

"Oh come on, Joelle. Would it be the end of the world if Brooke plays first base and you play...third base this time? It's good to play lots of different positions, you know."

"I guess," Joelle said. "I'm sure it'll work out. Your dad's a good coach. He'll do what's best for the team."

And that's the way Joelle wanted it.

As they turned onto her street, Joelle gasped. A familiar blue car was parked in their driveway.

"What's the matter?" Elizabeth asked.

"That's my brother's car!" Joelle said excitedly. "I've got to go, okay? I'll call you later."

"Okay," Elizabeth said, but Joelle was already bolting for home.

Jason was sitting on the porch out front. He had bleached the top part of his hair, but other than that he looked like the same old Jason. Tall and stick-figure thin with a smile that lit up his whole face. When he saw Joelle coming, he stood up.

"JASON!" Joelle screamed, throwing herself into his wiry arms.

Jason laughed as he hugged her back. "Hey, Jojo," he said. "Take it easy, okay?"

"What are you doing here? Why didn't you tell me you were coming? Do Mom and Dad know you're here?" Joelle asked, finally pulling away from him. But she couldn't let go of him completely. She clung to his arm with both hands.

Jason tugged on Joelle's ponytail. "Well, my chem lab was cancelled this afternoon, so I thought I'd come check out the new place. It was only a five-hour drive."

"So how long are you here for?" Joelle asked. "Can you stay the whole weekend?"

"Well, I have to work Sunday morning, so I'll head back late tomorrow afternoon," Jason replied.

Joelle frowned. She knew her brother had to work at Rocky's Pizza to help pay for college. But she hated that he had to leave so soon.

"You'll at least stay for our game tomorrow, won't you?" she asked. "It's in the morning."

"Game? What game?" Jason asked.

"It's a long story," Joelle said. As she showed her brother around their new house, she filled him in on everything that had been going on.

Jason flopped down on the familiar oversized couch in the family room. "Look at all this," he said, his glance taking in the large paneled room. "You've got a bigger house, new friends, and a whole new girls' baseball league."

Joelle sat down next to her brother and plopped her feet on the coffee table. "Yeah. And guess what? I'm doing some other stuff, too."

"Like what?" Jason raised his eyebrows.

"Well, I made second clarinet. And I might join the *Echo* next year. Can you believe it? *Me* on the newspaper staff? I never even *read* the school paper back in Minneapolis."

"Way to go, Pest," Jason said, chuckling.

"But the best thing is definitely the league," Joelle finished.

"I'm not surprised to hear it's taking off." Jason leaned back against the couch. "When you set your mind to something, Jojo, there's no stopping you."

"Just like you," Joelle said.

Jason looked at her for a minute. "No." He shook his head. "Not like me. Not like me at all."

Joelle nudged Jason with her foot. "What are you talking about? Aren't you Mr. Big Shot? Honor student, awesome baseball player, generally all-around amazing person?"

Jason looked surprised. "Not me." He picked up a red vase from the coffee table, turned it around in his hands, then set it back down. He didn't look at Joelle. "I would never start up a brand new baseball league."

"You would if it was the only way you could play," Joelle said.

Jason shook his head. "I don't think so," he said slowly. "To tell you the truth, if I'd have been in your shoes, I probably would have just played softball and not worried about it."

"You would not!" Joelle said.

"I would too!"

Joelle shifted on the couch. "Well, then, why'd you tell me to write that letter to the newspaper? 'Make them let you play,' you said. 'Let them see what you can do.' Why didn't you just tell me to play softball if that's what you would've done?"

"Because you're not me," Jason said. "You're not the kind of person who gives up. You always find another way, even if it's really hard. You never turn down a challenge."

"Neither do you," Joelle said.

Jason laughed self-consciously. "I turn down challenges all the time, Jojo. How do you think I made the honor roll all through high school?"

"Because you're smart," Joelle replied.

"Nope. I made the honor roll because I never took advanced math, chemistry, or physics. I only took the easy classes. The easier, the better. The less homework, the better. And now I'm paying for it in college."

"What do you mean?" Joelle frowned.

Jason looked away. "Well, my grades might be a little better now if I knew how to apply myself. I never really learned to work hard at something. I'm not like you. I always took the easy way out."

This was news to Joelle. "What about baseball?" she asked. "You work hard at baseball, right?"

Jason shrugged. "Baseball's different. I'm good at it, so it's not really work for me. Take the clarinet, for example." He turned back to Joelle. "I quit when it got too hard."

Joelle stared at her feet and rocked them slowly from side to side. Was all of this true? She didn't know what to say. This was a side of her brother she'd never seen before. Or maybe she'd just never noticed.

"I'm going to have to pull up my grades to stay on the team," Jason said. "But hey, I'll figure something out. Maybe I'll get a tutor or something."

"Oh." Joelle thought for a moment. "Well, hey, if you flunk out of college, you can always move in here," she said.

"Move to Iowa?" Jason grinned and pretended to shudder. "I don't think so."

"Oh, come on," Joelle said. "Iowa's not so bad." And to her surprise, she realized she actually meant it.

Chapter Twenty

*I*t *isn't exactly the Metrodome in downtown Minneapolis,* Joelle thought. *Or even the baseball field behind Hoover Middle School.* But at least the Green Sox and the Kernels had a place to play on Saturday morning.

Mrs. Holmes's lot was set back against the woods, but there was a large open area in front. The spot was perfect for a base-ball game. People gathered close together on blankets and folding chairs around the field, waiting for the game to start. It looked to Joelle like an even bigger crowd than last week.

Mrs. Holmes had a seat right in front. Next to her sat another older lady who also looked familiar. Was that Ms. Fenner's mom? Yes, Joelle was sure it was. The two women seemed to know each other.

Wow, Joelle thought. *All of these people came to see the Green Sox and the Kernels play ball.*

"So do you think anybody's going to kick us off the field this week?" Tara asked as she adjusted the sizing on her green cap.

"Just let them try," Brooke replied. "This time we're play-ing on private property."

"Hey, Channel 6 is here again!" Nikki pointed at the TV crew that was setting up behind the field.

Joelle noticed that Ryan Carlyle was here again, too. And this time, so was his dad. What was he doing here?

"Okay, Green Sox, listen up," Coach Shaw said as he gathered the team together in the makeshift dugout. Coach Kennedy was talking to her players on the other side of the field. The Kernels were dressed in black pants and yellow shirts. "As far as I know, this is the first time there's been a game between two all-girls' baseball teams around here," Coach Shaw said. "You should be very proud of everything you've done to get this far."

Joelle glanced around at her new friends. She *was* proud. Very proud. Of all of them.

"Remember, it doesn't matter whether we win or lose," Coach Shaw continued. "We're just here to play—and have fun."

He went on to explain how things would work. They would play six innings, just like Little League. The coaches would umpire.

Finally, Coach Shaw began to assign fielding positions. "Okay, let's see," he said. "We'll have Mandi as pitcher and Nikki as catcher."

Joelle crossed her fingers inside her mitt. *Me at first base,* she begged silently. *Please please please.*

"And Joelle at first base," Coach Shaw went on.

Yes!

Joelle was about to jump up in celebration. Then she remembered Brooke.

But Brooke just grinned good-naturedly and gave Joelle a thumbs-up.

"Leah at second and Tara at third. Brooke's at shortstop. Page, you're left field; Paula, center field; and Elizabeth, right field."

So Brooke was going to play shortstop. She didn't seem disappointed at all. In fact, she actually looked happy.

That made Joelle feel better. They were a real team now. They were all going to have to work together.

Coach Kennedy walked over just as Coach Shaw finished talking. She had a bright smile on her face. "Should we toss a coin to see who's up first?"

"Sure." Coach Shaw pulled a coin out of his front jeans pocket. "You want to call it?"

"No. The Kernels took a vote. We decided Joelle Cunningham should call it, since this whole league was her idea."

"Wow. Really?" As far as Joelle was concerned, she'd had a lot of help. They'd all done it together.

Mandi shoved Joelle forward. "Come on, Joelle. We don't have all day. Call it."

Joelle nodded. "Okay," she said. "Heads."

Coach Shaw flipped the coin, caught it, and slapped it to his arm. "Sorry," he said. "It's tails."

The Kernels chose to bat last.

The two coaches talked for a bit, then signaled their teams to take the field. Everyone in the crowd quieted down. Both coaches thanked everyone for coming and introduced their players.

People applauded and whistled as each name was called. When the coach said her name, Joelle heard her parents and brother cheering. She thought she recognized Ryan's voice, too.

Finally someone yelled, "Play ball!" The crowd started clapping and shouting even louder.

"You're the lead-off batter, Joelle," Coach Shaw said.

Joelle picked up the bat, took a couple of practice swings, and got into position. She felt good. Really good. "Come on, Joelle!" her teammates called.

The girl on the pitcher's mound looked as if she meant business. She wound up and pitched a fastball straight down the center.

Crack! Joelle hit a line drive between first and second base.

"Run, Joelle! Run!" the Green Sox cheered.

Joelle bolted toward first. She stopped there after overrunning the base.

"Way to go!" Coach Shaw clapped as Joelle walked back to the bag. "Base hit."

Nikki was up next. "Go for it, Nikki!" Joelle shouted. She took a short lead.

The pitch was high and wide.

"Ball one," Coach Kennedy called.

The next pitch was a strike. Then another ball. And finally strike three. Nikki was out. Her face fell.

"It's okay, Nikki! You'll do it next time!" Brooke called as Mandi stepped up to bat. The rest of the Green Sox clapped.

On the first pitch, Mandi slammed the ball out to left field. Joelle rounded second base and kept going. The fielder threw the ball to the third baseman, but Joelle slid under it.

"Safe!" Coach Kennedy shouted.

"All right, Joelle!" someone shouted from the stands. Joelle was sure she recognized Ryan's voice this time.

Mandi waved to Joelle from second base. Joelle grinned and waved back.

Tara was up next. Tara was a powerful hitter. But the first pitch was too low. She swung anyway.

"Strike one!" Coach Shaw called.

The next pitch was low, too. Tara swung again.

"Strike two!" Coach Shaw called.

Joelle frowned. She really wanted to make it home this first inning. That would be a perfect start for the new league. "Come on, Tara!" she shouted.

The third pitch was also low. But this time Tara connected with it. Joelle didn't even watch where it went. She took off for home.

"Go! Go! Go!" The Green Sox were jumping up and down. "Yes!" they all screamed when Joelle crossed the bag.

The Kernels outfielder had missed the ball, so both Mandi and Tara came in, too.

"Way to go, Tara!" Joelle shouted as Tara crossed the plate.

After that, Leah struck out. And Paula was thrown out at first to retire the side. But all in all, it was a great start.

"Come on, Mandi," Joelle clapped her friend on the back as they headed out to the field. "Show them what you're made of."

"Don't worry, I will." Mandi gave the ball a toss in her mitt.

She struck out the first three batters in order. One, two, three.

At the end of the first inning, the score was Green Sox 3, Kernels 0. Somebody in the stands whistled sharply.

Hopefully this game won't be too *easy,* Joelle thought. She wanted to win, of course, but she wanted to work for it a little, too. Besides, the crowd always liked a close score.

As the game went on, the Kernels pitcher learned how to handle the Green Sox. In the third inning, she struck out Paula, Tara, and Leah. And the next time when the Kernels were up, they scored three runs.

"We're tied now," Nikki moaned as the Green Sox headed back to the dugout.

"That's okay. We'll score again this inning," Joelle said confidently as she wiped her forehead with a towel.

Luckily, they did. Elizabeth scored a run. She was so excited she ran over and hugged her dad after she crossed home plate.

"Way to go, honey!" he said as Elizabeth laughed and jumped around. "That's my little slugger."

"Dad!" Elizabeth stopped jumping. Her face was as red as her hair. The Kernels scored two more runs that inning, too, which put them one ahead of the Green Sox.

"Give it up, Green Sox!" one of the Kernels called as the two teams switched places at the top of the fifth.

"Try and make us," Tara shot back.

The Green Sox dropped their gloves, grabbed their water bottles, and plopped down on the bench.

"Hey, look. It's not just Channel 6 that's here!" Brooke

noticed as Paige went up to bat. "Channel 9 from Cedar Rapids came, too! Wow."

All the girls turned. Sure enough, there was a tall guy in a baseball cap standing on the other side of the fence behind third base. He carried a large camera with the Channel 9 logo on his shoulder.

"He's filming us!" Mandi squealed.

"People all over Eastern Iowa get Channel 9!" Leah exclaimed.

"Come on, Paige!" Brooke called. "Let's score this inning. We want to look good on TV!"

Paige struck out. But the Green Sox scored three runs that inning, bringing their total to 7. The Kernels closed out the inning at 5.

The Green Sox scored one more run in the sixth. Then it was the Kernels' final turn at bat.

"Come on, Mandi," Nikki said, "Strike 'em out, one, two, three. Just like you did in the first inning."

"I'll try," Mandi said.

She struck out the first two batters easily, but the third batter nicked the ball as it made its way to Nikki's mitt.

"Strike one!" Coach Shaw called.

Mandi wound up and fired again. The batter swung. The ball went down the foul line and bounced out of bounds. "Strike two!" Coach Shaw called.

"Come on, Mandi," Joelle yelled. "Just one more."

Mandi paused. Then she stepped forward and fired the ball with all her might. It sailed straight into Nikki's mitt.

"Strike three!"

That was it. The game was over. The Green Sox had won, 8–5.

All the Green Sox and Kernels players ran out on the field. "Good game! Good game!" They passed each other in two long lines, shaking hands.

The crew from Channel 9 recorded the whole thing. A newscaster Joelle recognized from billboards all over town whipped out a microphone, put on a wide smile, and said for the camera, "This is Lydia Morris. I'm here with the Greendale Green Sox and the Chesterfield Kernels after a truly exciting ball game. That's *base*ball, folks."

Joelle and Elizabeth exchanged glances. The way the news-caster said "exciting," you'd think she'd played in the game herself.

"I want to point out to all you viewers that these are all-female baseball teams. No boys allowed, right, girls?" Lydia smiled again for the people at home.

"Yep, girls only," said one of the Kernels.

"So what's it like playing on an all-girls' baseball team?" Lydia thrust her microphone in Leah's face.

Leah stepped back a little. "It's uh…great," she said, obviously unprepared.

"The Eastern Iowa Girls' Baseball League rocks!" Nikki called out loudly from the back of the crowd.

All of the girls laughed and cheered.

"But we need more players," Brooke added, stepping forward. "Come join the Green Sox!"

One of the Kernels next to her gave her a playful shove. "Join the Kernels!" she said, shouting into the microphone.

Lydia took a few comments from the coaches and from Mrs. Holmes and Mrs. Fenner. Then she finished her report by urging anyone who was interested in playing or helping out with the new girls' baseball league to contact either Coach Shaw or Coach Kennedy.

Still beaming, Joelle turned to see if her family was anywhere in sight. But she suddenly found herself face to face with Coach Carlyle. And Ryan.

Joelle's glove slipped from her hands. "Uh, hi, Co— I mean, Mr. Carlyle," she said as she bent to pick up her glove. Her heart was pounding harder now than it had during the game.

Coach Carlyle just looked at her and nodded. "Good game," he said finally.

"Thanks," Joelle said carefully.

Coach Carlyle started to move on, but Ryan hung back. "I think I see now why you wanted to do this rather than play for the Hawks," he said.

"Really?" Joelle said in surprise.

Ryan grinned. "Yeah. This baseball league of yours is *big!* Practically the whole town is here!"

Joelle grinned back. What could she say? It was true.

* * *

"It's so weird," Joelle said to Jason as she leaned against his car later that afternoon. "Before we moved to Greendale, I never even thought about playing on an all-girls' baseball team."

Jason tossed his duffel bag into the trunk. "And now you actually helped form one," he said. "Way to go, Jojo."

"We're all proud of you," their dad said, coming up and putting an arm around Joelle.

"I guess I'll have to get started on a women's league now," Mom said.

"Just let me know if you need any pointers, Mom," Joelle teased.

Jason walked around to the side of his car. "So, do you still want to come back to Minneapolis and move in with me?" he asked Joelle. He held open the door. "Hop in, Pest."

"Move in with *you?*" Joelle cried. "Are you crazy? You're a total slob!"

They all laughed.

Jason turned to hug Mom and Dad, then Joelle. "See, I told you things would work out," he said.

"I still wish you were here with us, too," she said. "Then everything would be perfect."

"I'm not that far away," Jason said. "And I'll be back for the summer. I'll call you, okay?"

Joelle grinned. "Yeah, sure you will."

As she stood on the front porch with her parents, waving good-bye to Jason, she thought about how much things had changed lately.

She'd thought moving to Greendale was the end of the world. But instead it turned out to be just the beginning.

Things were going to be okay here, Joelle could tell. And if something suddenly *wasn't* okay...well, then she would just have to *do* something about it.

Author's Note

Sliding into Home is a work of fiction. Greendale is not a real town. Joelle and her friends are not real people. But Joelle's situation is very real.

I got the idea for this book when I read a newspaper article in the late 1990s about a young girl who wasn't allowed to play baseball. Intrigued with her story, I looked on the internet to find more information. During my search, I discovered that other girls who wanted to play baseball had been told no. Girls all across the country are *still* being told no.

When I looked back at the history of baseball, I couldn't understand why young women would ever be denied the chance to play. Women have been playing baseball since the game was invented. Vassar College, a prestigious all-women's institution, was founded in 1865. Within a year, Vassar had two baseball teams. Shortly thereafter, several other women's colleges also had baseball teams. The players wore long-sleeved shirts with high necklines, wide skirts that hung to the ground, and high-button shoes. But it wasn't long before disapproving mothers forced all of these early teams to disband!

During World War II, while many of the male Major League ball players were off fighting in Europe and the Pacific, the All-American Professional Girls Baseball League was formed. Young women played in this league from 1943 until 1954. The popular 1992 movie *A League of Their Own* was based on these players' experiences.

Today there are more than twenty-three all-women's base-ball teams throughout the world. As of this writing, the Women's Baseball League (www.baseballglory.com) is in the process of obtaining approval for the American Athletic Union (www.aausports.org) to sanction girls' baseball in the United States.

The Pawtucket Slaterettes Girls Baseball League in Pawtucket, Rhode Island is a real girls' baseball league. And they really do have a website at www.slaterettes.com. This league has been around since 1973, when nine-year-old Pookie Fortin wanted to play baseball with the Pawtucket Darlington American Little League (DALL). That organization did not allow girls to play on their teams and refused to let her join the league. The young girl's family took DALL to court. Pookie never did play for DALL, but her situation led to the formation of the Pawtucket Slaterettes Girls Baseball League.

Perhaps there will come a day when *any* girl who wants to play baseball will be able to. The Women's Sports Foundation (www.womenssportsfoundation.org), is another organization that is working toward that goal.

While writing this book, I corresponded with several girls around the country who were eager to play ball but couldn't, for one reason or another. I hope to hear soon from girls whose baseball dreams have come true.

We all have dreams—and that's what *Sliding into Home* is really about!

—D. H. B.